NANNY FOR THE MILLIONAIRE'S TWINS

BY

SUSAN MEIER

All the characters in this book have no existence outside the imagination of the author, and have no relation whatsoever to anyone bearing the same name or names. They are not even distantly inspired by any individual known or unknown to the author, and all the incidents are pure invention.

First published in Great Britain 2012
by Mills & Boon, an imprint of Harlequin (UK) Limited.
Large Print edition 2013
Harlequin (UK) Limited, Eton House,
18-24 Paradise Road, Richmond, Surrey TW9 1SR

ISBN: 978 0 263 23165 6

Harlequin (UK) policy is to use papers that are natural, renewable and recyclable products and made from wood grown in sustainable forests. The logging and manufacturing process conform to the legal environmental regulations of the country of origin.

Printed and bound in Great Britain
by CPI Antony Rowe, Chippenham, Wiltshire

For the hospice patients
and their wonderful families who have
taught me in my years of volunteering that
the truth about life and death, love and hope,
is sometimes very simple.

CHAPTER ONE

CHANCE MONTGOMERY PULLED his SUV up to the big black iron gates that protected his mother's estate. He punched in the code she'd given him, and, after the gates opened, drove along the winding lane, not surprised that nothing had changed. The leaves on the tall trees that lead to the mansion had turned red, yellow and orange, the way they always did in October in Pine Ward, Pennsylvania. The brown and gray stone mansion, his childhood home, looked exactly as it had on his eighteenth birthday, when he'd run away.

He'd left because his life was a mess. A rope of days, months and years braided together with betrayal and lies. Ironically, he was returning for the same reason. The woman he'd thought was the love of his life had left him when she realized she was pregnant with his twins. She'd never loved him, only used him as a stepping stone to get where she wanted to be in her career. Nine months later, she'd had their babies and seemed to mother them adequately for six or so months. Then suddenly two weeks ago, she'd brought them to his house and said she didn't want them back.

Odd that it took her giving up the kids to reinforce the valuable lesson he'd learned when he'd discovered his adoptive father was actually his biological father. People couldn't be trusted. Most looked out for themselves. He should have remembered that when she told him she'd only been with him to use him. But, no. He'd actually held out hope that even if she didn't love him, she could love their kids.

He was an idiot.

He pulled the SUV in front of one of the garage doors, clicked off the ignition and jumped out. As if she'd been waiting for him, his mom hurried over.

"Chance, darling!" Her snow-white hair was cut short in a neat and elegant style. Her black trousers and black turtleneck with pearls made her look like the socialite that she was.

She enfolded him in the kind of embrace only a mother can pull off without looking foolish.

When she stepped away, her eyes were filled with tears. "I'm so glad you're home."

He cleared his throat. He wished he could say the same, but the truth was he wasn't happy to be here. He wasn't happy he couldn't handle his twins. He wasn't happy his babies' mother didn't want to be in their lives. He wasn't happy that every person in his life hurt him, cheated him or lied to him.

Except Gwen Montgomery. The devoted wife his father had tricked into adopting him. A woman who, even once she'd found out he was her husband's illegitimate son, hadn't stopped loving him.

"It's good to be home."

Okay. That was a bit of a lie. But how could he tell the happy woman in front of him the truth? That this house reminded him of a dad who couldn't be trusted. That his life sucked…

He couldn't.

She clapped her hands together. "So let me see them!"

He reached for the back door of the SUV just as a tall redhead walked out of the mansion. He would have been lying if he said he didn't notice her face was pretty. Big brown eyes, a pert nose and full, lush lips always added up to pretty. But she wore a plain white blouse, gray pants and ugly—truly ugly—black shoes.

His mother said, "By the way, this is Victoria Bingham. She likes to be called Tory. I hired her to be your nanny."

Normally, he would have reached over and taken the hand she extended to shake his. Instead, he turned to his mom. "I told you, Mom, I want to raise the kids myself. I came here for help from you, not an outsider."

Gwen straightened as if he'd mortally wounded her. "Well, of course, I'll help you. But you also need a nanny for things like diapers—"

"I can change diapers. I've changed thirty thousand in the past two weeks. These kids were abandoned by their mom. They're not going to lose their daddy too."

She laid her hand on his cheek. "Oh, darling. We are not going to let these kids go without love. You had a nanny until you were four. And you don't think I love you any less than a baby raised without a nanny, do you?"

He shook his head. Gwen's love had been

proven a million times over when she accepted her husband's infidelity a lot better than Chance had.

"So, you see? Nannies are perfectly suitable help."

He mumbled, "I suppose," turned to the SUV door, opened it and revealed his two true pride and joys. Little bruiser Sam yelped indignantly as if he resented being stuck in his car seat while everybody else talked. Cindy gurgled happily.

"Oh, darling! They're gorgeous!"

They were gorgeous.

Standing off to the side, Tory Bingham stared at the two blond-haired, blue-eyed babies. She hadn't wanted this job. After years of surgeries and the resultant therapies to repair her left leg, which had been shattered in a motorcycle accident, she could finally walk with the support of orthopedic shoes. She could also drive. Her plan had been to spend her days with her fiancé, who hadn't fared as well as she had after their accident. But her parents had other ideas.

They wanted her to get a job. Worse, they wanted her to get on with her life. While her fiancé lay in a personal care facility struggling, they wanted her to move on. It wasn't just ridiculous; it was horrific.

But she was twenty-five years old. She didn't have any money. She didn't have health insurance. All of her medical expenses had been picked up by Jason's motorcycle insurance, but she was reaching even those limits. Her parents might be friends of the Montgomerys but they didn't have the money the Montgomery family had. She had no choice but to take the job Gwen had offered.

And now the prodigal son didn't want her.

Fine with her. She would find work somewhere else. Except…

Well, his babies *were* adorable. The two sweet angels sitting in bear-print car seats caused an unexpected tumble of her heart, and she couldn't stop staring at them.

Chance ducked into the SUV. "Here, I'll get them out."

"That's okay." Gwen scurried around the trailer hitched to the back of the SUV—the trailer hauling a big black motorcycle. "You get Sam. I'll get Cindy."

She opened the door and leaned in to get the little girl, but within a few seconds, she pulled out again. "Tory, can you help me with these strap things? I can't seem to get them unbuckled."

Tory said, "Yes, ma'am," and hurried around the trailer. Apparently she wasn't being fired after all.

But even staying as far away as she could from the black beast on the trailer, her chest tightened with terror as she maneuvered around it. She remembered her motorcycle accident as something like a soundless blur that flashed into her brain at the oddest times of the day and night. A blur that had all but destroyed her leg and nearly taken the man she loved.

"Hurry, Tory!"

Tory scooted to the SUV door, dipped in to undo the buckle and found herself six inches away from the most adorable face in the universe. Big blue eyes blinked at her. Cherubic lips blew spit bubbles. "Well, hello, there."

The baby gurgled with happiness.

"Aren't you just the sweetest little thing?" She undid the last buckle and lifted the baby out of her seat.

For the first time since the accident, Tory's chest expanded with delight. The baby patted her face and she laughed. But Gwen eagerly waited to hold the little girl and Tory handed her over.

"Well, my goodness," Gwen said. "It is a pleasure to meet you, Cindy. I'm your grandmother."

Tory's eyebrows rose. Gwen had never met her own grandchildren? She knew Chance had been away for a while, but she'd thought they'd reconciled.

Gwen walked around the trailer again. "Come on. Let's get them into the house."

"Actually, Mom—" Chance winced. "One whiff of Sam and I can tell he needs to be changed. Maybe we should just take them directly to the cottage?"

His mom's face fell. "Oh."

"It's been a long drive and once I change them I should feed them."

Gwen smiled as if she was so happy to have her son home she would agree to anything. "Okay. Tory and I will come with you."

He glanced over at Tory and she looked back at him. She'd already noticed he was tall and lean. That his hair was black and his eyes were blue. That a red flannel shirt suited him and so did butt-molding jeans. But holding the gaze of his blue eyes, she saw other things. Subtleties. Those pretty sapphire eyes had the wariness of a man who didn't trust.

Which was just perfect. She hadn't ever worked full-time beyond the job of watching kids for three summers when she was in high school, and now her first real nanny job came with a distrustful father.

Well, she wasn't going to beg him to keep her or even defend herself. She didn't really want to work for a grouch. Especially not a grouch she didn't know. Nannies lived with the family who employed them. If he kept her, she'd be spending twenty-four hours a day with him.

"Just think, Chance," Gwen said teasingly. "If you have a nanny, you don't have to get up with the twins in the middle of the night—and, even if you do, you only have to change and feed one baby."

He rubbed his hand along the back of his neck, as if bone tired and finding it hard to refute that argument. "All right. You both can come."

After they strapped the kids into their seats,

Tory sat between the twins so Gwen could ride in the front with her son.

As they made their way down the slim brown brick lane that wound through the forest behind Gwen's mansion, Tory began to see just how private their living arrangements would be. The trees were thick enough that it was nearly dark. Only occasionally did light pierce the red, yellow and orange leafy overhangs and create shiny beams that sparkled to the ground.

She swallowed. Maybe her first instincts had been correct? Maybe she should have held her ground with her mom and told her she didn't want a job. She wanted to be with Jason, to take care of him, to help him recover. Not trapped in a secluded cottage with a man she didn't know.

They stopped in front of a one-story house too big to be called a cottage. Though it was stone and had adorable windows and a roof with several peaks, it was obviously roomy and modern.

Gwen led them through the great room to the bedroom she'd had redesigned and furnished as a nursery. Two oak cribs, two changing tables and two rockers filled it.

Chance laid chubby Sam on the first changing table. Gwen set Cindy on the second. "Tory, darling, while we're changing the diapers, could you make the babies some cereal?"

"Sure." Happy to escape, she raced outside to the SUV, assuming she'd find baby supplies there. But all she saw were two duffle bags. When she brought them into the kitchen and rummaged through them, she found nothing but clothes.

"See anything you like?"

Her heart just about leaped out of her chest at Chance's question. His voice was low and deep, and the sexy way he folded his arms across his chest and leaned against the center island of the kitchen caused her pulse to scramble.

Annoyance skittered through her. Why did she keep noticing things about this man? She was engaged. She shouldn't be looking at his handsome face or noting the way he moved. Plus, at first blush, she didn't even like him.

Presenting him with what she hoped was a professional smile, she said, "I was looking for cereal."

He handed her the diaper bag. "It's in here. Mom said she had the refrigerator stocked with supplies, including milk. Use that since mine's been sitting in this diaper bag for hours."

With that he turned and walked away, and Tory let out the breath she didn't even realize she was holding. He might be good-looking but he was crabby. Even if she wasn't engaged, she shouldn't be interested—attracted, whatever the devil she was—to him.

She quickly prepared the cereal. By the time she carried it into the nursery, Chance and his mom were on the rocking chairs, each holding a baby. She put the two small bowls on the round table between the rockers and stepped back. Chance fed little bruiser Sam and Gwen fed Cindy.

With nothing else to do, she stood by the door and watched them. Though the babies were twins and looked a bit alike, they weren't identical. Aside from their disparate size, they had different hair. Sam's was short and fine, but Cindy's was thick and longer. Yellow curls fell to her forehead and along her nape.

When they were done, Chance rose from his rocker. "I think we should put them down for a nap. They've eaten and now they'll be tired."

"So it's not their regularly scheduled nap time?" Gwen asked.

He snorted a laugh. "Scheduled nap time? I don't tell them when to sleep or eat. They tell me."

Remembering the trouble she'd had her first summer with the Perkins family, wealthy lawyers with kids who ran roughshod over them, Tory couldn't stifle the, "Oh, dear" that escaped her lips.

She instantly regretted it. Chance's pretty blue eyes narrowed at her and his mouth thinned into an angry line.

He patted Sam's back a bit, then laid the drowsy child in the crib. Following Chance's lead, Gwen did the same with Cindy. The babies fell asleep instantly and Chance headed for the door, his mom on his heels.

Tory followed them out of the nursery, wanting to kick herself. The guy already didn't like her and she didn't exactly like him. Did she have to make things worse with her big mouth?

When they reentered the main room, Gwen turned to Chance. "Since the babies are sleeping, there's no point in us hanging around. Plus, you and I could use a little catch up time." She smiled at him. "Why don't you drive us back to the house and we'll go to the den where there's good brandy? We can have Cook make us a snack."

Chance pulled his keys from his jeans pocket again. He caught Tory's gaze. "Watch the kids."

She nodded, as relief washed over her. Hopefully, he and his mom would chitchat long enough that she could figure out a way to quit gracefully since their mothers were friends. He didn't want her and she didn't want to work for him. This wasn't rocket science. But she also wouldn't put her mom or Gwen in an uncomfortable position over a failed nanny assignment.

After they left, Tory relaxed and roamed the cottage. She'd been so preoccupied with Chance and the cereal, that she hadn't really taken a good look at the house. The three bedrooms were in the back, but the living space had an open floor plan. Standing in the yellow kitchen with maple cabinets, beige ceramic tile floor and brown and beige granite countertops, she could see the entire family room and the mini-library/reading area behind it. A table and chairs sat off to the left of the kitchen in a little space that looked like a sunroom because of all the windows.

It was the perfect home for a young family—or newlyweds. She ran her hand along the granite countertop. She should be married right now. Living in a cute little house like this. Raising her own babies. But one day…one hour… No, one *minute* had changed everything. Instead of being married, being a mom, or having a career, she spent hours on end in a hospital room, talking to a fiancé who couldn't talk back.

She wasn't even really sure he could hear her.

Forcing herself out of her dark mood, she walked to the sitting area with the oversize leather sofa and recliners and big-screen TV, and turned in a circle. For a "cottage" this was unbelievable.

"So now you're dancing?"

She spun to face Chance as he walked in the front door. "I was just exploring a bit." Pressing her hand to her galloping heart, she tried to level her breathing. "I thought you were visiting with your mom."

"I'm not leaving my babies indefinitely with a stranger."

"I'm not a stranger. Our mothers are friends.

Plus, I've been living with your mom, working with the household staff for a week."

"And one would think you would have learned your place."

She sucked in a breath. Oh, boy. The moment of truth. She might not have to figure out how to quit gracefully. He might fire her before she could.

He motioned for her to sit on the sofa. "You and I need to talk."

Resigned, she walked over and sat on the couch as he'd requested.

He plopped down on one of the recliners. "You crossed a line when you questioned me about the kids' nap time."

She winced. "Technically, I didn't question you. I said, 'oh, dear.'"

"Which is worse. You might as well have come right out and said, 'Hey, Chance. You're doing everything wrong.'"

"Sorry."

"These are my kids. I've spent two weeks with them all by myself. And though I'm not perfect, I don't want to be constantly reminded that I don't always know what I'm doing."

Her head snapped up. He didn't know what he was doing? He had *twins* and he didn't know what he was doing?

"I didn't hire a nanny because I want my kids to be raised by me. But I'm willing to give you a shot because quite honestly I could use some help. Plus, I'm not staying here forever. Only for a visit."

Only for a visit? Her attention perked up even more. If he wasn't staying forever, only for a visit, then this job was temporary. She wasn't making a life decision or a life choice or even abandoning Jason. She was working temporarily.

Giddy relief swamped her.

"But I have to tell you, if you're going to criticize me, we can end this right now."

With her situation in perspective, she studied him as all the puzzle pieces of *his* situation began to fall into place in her head. Gwen had told her that the twins' mother had left his babies with him, saying she didn't want them back—which explained his trust issues. He didn't want a nanny. He wanted to raise these kids on his own. Admirable. But he didn't know how. And because he was sort of failing he was supersensitive.

He wasn't a grouch. Just a supersensitive daddy who needed somebody to help him.

Suddenly being that person didn't seem so god-awful.

"Are we clear?"

Crystal. "Yes."

"Great." Even as he said the word, one of the babies began to cry. He rose from his seat.

Tory also rose. Okay. She might not be quitting. But the job was far from perfect. She still wasn't sure she could advise him without insulting him.

Walking to the nursery he said, "Here's the only reason I might not—and I stress *might not*—mind having you around. I can't seem to get Sam and Cindy to sleep for more than twenty minutes, and when they get up they're like little cats climbing all over me. I don't get a minute's peace."

"You've been holding these kids for two weeks?"

"Sort of. Sometimes they play on the floor."

"What about your job?"

"I own a construction company so I could pretty much do what I wanted for the first week. But once I realized I had my hands full with the kids, I turned everything over to my general manager."

She carefully caught his gaze. His blue eyes were no longer angry, but cautious. "You can't live like that forever."

He sniffed a laugh. "No kidding."

"Yet, you don't want a nanny."

"I don't want to be like my dad."

"He never had time for you?"

He sighed, ran his fingers through his short dark hair. "These kids are just adjusting to losing their mom. I can't leave them too."

Gorgeous or not, grouchy or not, deep down inside Chance Montgomery was a nice guy. And he genuinely loved his kids. Surely she could put her own problems on hold long enough to help him. Especially when she needed to earn a little money as much as he needed assistance with his kids.

She cautiously said, "So you want suggestions about some things?"

He sighed. "When I ask? Yes."

"Are you asking?"

His sigh turned into a growl. "The fact that you

think I should be asking means I should be, so, yes, I'm asking."

"I didn't see a baby swing or a walker in your car—"

"A walker?" His brow furrowed and he looked at her as if she were crazy. "Like an old person's walker?"

If he hadn't been so serious, she might have laughed. But if he didn't even know what a swing and a walker were, then chances were he hadn't forgotten to pack them for this trip. He didn't have them. Which heaped another layer of trouble onto his already troubled daddyhood.

Not wanting to insult him, she carefully said, "A walker is a seat with wheels that you put your babies in. It helps them learn to walk, but it also entertains them."

"You mean they don't have to spend every waking minute crawling on me?"

His hopeful tone broke her heart. "Nope."

"And I suppose the swing is something every bit as useful?"

She winced then nodded. "I'm amazed your ex-wife didn't give you those things when she gave you the kids."

"Liliah wasn't my wife. She isn't going to be anybody's wife. And as you can see, she took real well to mothering too."

He turned and headed for the nursery and Tory squeezed her eyes shut in misery.

Just when it looked like they might have been starting to get along, she said something stupid.

This was never going to work.

CHAPTER TWO

REACHING IN TO lift Sam out of his crib, Chance stopped the anger rolling through him. He shouldn't be surprised that Liliah hadn't given him all the things the kids needed. But with a screaming baby on his shoulder and a woman who seemed to know what she was doing standing right behind him, this wasn't the time to let his brain tumble to his anger with Liliah.

"So why do you think they woke up?"

Tory walked to Cindy's crib. Chance's sobbing little girl raised her arms, begging to be held. "Did they sleep on the drive here?"

"Yes."

"Okay. So they probably just nodded off after you fed them because their tummies were full. They don't need a nap." She lifted Cindy out of her crib. "Hey, sweetie."

Cindy's sobbing subsided, and Chance watched as a look of wonder transformed Tory's features.

Her brown eyes lit with joy, and for the first time in weeks he felt himself begin to relax. Not only did she know what to do, but she truly seemed to love babies. Maybe a nanny wasn't such a bad idea after all?

"So they want to play?"

She rubbed her cheek against Cindy's. "Probably."

But as soon as she said the word, she winced. "You know, with these two up, and us really not having a whole heck of a lot of toys or anything to entertain them, maybe we should take a drive into town and get some supplies."

"Like that walker thing?"

"And a play yard and swings."

New guilt welled up in him. He was such an idiot. Couldn't he at least have thought of some of this stuff? Was he that dumb that he couldn't draw some commonsense conclusions?

No. Actually, he wasn't dumb as much as tired. So tired from being up most of the night every night for the past two weeks that he hadn't been thinking straight.

"If we get them what they need and even a few toys, we'll be able to tire them out, and they'll actually sleep for longer stretches of time." She smiled tentatively. "They're old enough that we might even be able to train them to sleep through the night."

He looked longingly at her. "Really?"

She laughed and the soft sound hit him right in the gut. He told himself that was only because he wanted to be able to laugh again too. But she was pretty. Maybe even prettier than the women he used to date because she didn't seem to be wearing makeup. She didn't need it.

"Yeah. So grab your wallet and I'll get the diaper bag and we'll make a quick run to the store."

Thinking only of a full night's sleep, Chance buckled the kids in their car seats and headed for the mall on the outskirts of town. When they arrived, he flicked the switch signaling a turn into the mall parking lot, but Tory tapped his forearm and pointed at the discount department store.

"Let's go there. The quality is as good and you'll spend less money."

He did as she asked but as they got the kids out of the SUV, he sneaked a peek across the backseat at her. Usually, most of the women he met flirted outrageously with him and were impressed by his money. This one barely tolerated him and was now showing him how to save rather than spend?

Of course, she was an employee.

She wasn't interested in him as a man, or potential date, just as a boss.

That gave him a tug of something he couldn't quite identify. He suspected it was disappointment. But at this point he'd much rather have somebody good with the kids, than somebody to sleep with.

He almost laughed. Having two babies to care for certainly changed a man's priorities.

Automatic doors welcomed them into the store. Tory instructed him to get a cart and put Sam in the baby seat. Then she got a cart and put Cindy in that baby seat. They strolled past the rows and rows of everything from clothes and underwear to home goods and gardening tools until they came to the baby section.

She stopped her cart. "The most important things today are two walkers, two baby swings, a stroller for twins and one really strong play yard."

"Play yard?" She'd mentioned that before, but he didn't know what it was.

"Back in the day, moms called them playpens. We've gotten more politically correct and call them play yards now. It's a square thing like a box with mesh walls that you put the babies in so that they can play together but not crawl around and get into trouble."

He said, "Ah," and watched as she loaded a compact box into his cart. "I take it there's going to be some assembly required."

She winced. "Unfortunately. Maybe we can call Robert?" she said, referring to the groundskeeper.

He gaped at her. "I worked in construction for ten years before I started my own company, and even then I had to work with the crew sometimes." For some unknown reason his chest puffed out with pride. "I think I can handle putting together a playpen."

"Play yard," she corrected, as she loaded another big box into his cart.

"Play yard."

Unexpected happiness stole over him, loosened his tight chest, relaxed his stiff muscles. Not only would he get a reasonable night's sleep tonight, but his kids would be well cared for.

Not that he was a bad dad. If effort alone counted, he was daddy of the year. But effort hadn't counted. Otherwise, he'd have known about the walker, play yard and swing.

He paid for the purchases and loaded them into his SUV as Tory put first Cindy, then Sam, into their car seats. She explained more about the walker as they drove home. When they arrived, she had him assemble the swings as she popped two jars of baby food and fed the kids, using highchairs his mother had bought for the kitchen.

He had the swings together by the time she was done feeding and then cleaning up the kids, and they slid both inside. She wound what looked to be a music box for each one and voilà, suddenly both kids were swinging and happy.

"Wow. That is amazing."

"I'm surprised you didn't know about swings."

He gaped at her. "Who was I going to ask? I've only been talking to my mom again for a week and when she found out I had kids she just wanted me to come home."

"And she'd hired you a nanny."

"And she'd hired a nanny."

"So maybe your mom's a lot smarter than you give her credit for?"

He laughed.

She smiled.

And the room got quiet. The only sound was the music coming from the boxes and the creak of the kids' swings. The happiness and relief Chance had been feeling suddenly disappeared and were replaced by tightness and anticipation. He *liked* her.

He struggled with a sigh. Of course he liked her! She was helping him with his kids. And she was beautiful and he hadn't been around a woman "that way" since Liliah—which, counting her pregnancy was fifteen months ago. Fifteen months without a date? Sheesh. Liliah had really done a number on him.

But because she had, he wasn't interested in a relationship. If he was going to have a woman in his life, it would strictly be for fun. No more potential heartaches. No more bitter fights. Just… fun. And a smart man didn't get involved with his nanny just for fun.

Especially not when he desperately needed her.

He moved his gaze away from hers and pointed at the swing. "So they're good for what? Twenty minutes in this thing?"

"They can actually stay in longer. I've heard of moms letting their kids nap in there."

"It's like a miracle."

"Well, spending hours in a swing can't be good for a baby's back. But once they're out of the swing—" She bent and grabbed some plastic toys. "You put them in the play yard with a few of these and see what happens. Lots of times babies will entertain themselves if you let them."

He took a breath, said the word that had been choking in his chest all afternoon. "Thanks."

She glanced up at him with a smile. "You're welcome."

But her smile quickly faded. So did his. Those male feelings swept over him again. She was so pretty. And the babies were so quiet, he felt like himself again. A man. Not just a daddy. She was attracted to him. He knew she was attracted to him. Her face told the story. It would be perfectly natural to start flirting right now…

He stopped his thoughts. Stepped back.

He'd already thought all this out. He didn't want

a relationship. He absolutely wasn't going let another woman get close enough to hurt him—or the twins. And if he had no intention of getting close, then the only thing flirting would lead to was a fling.

That was just wrong.

He rubbed his hand along the back of his neck. "Your supper never did come down from the main house."

She took a pace back too. "I know." She cleared her throat. "Think you'll be okay while I go up and check on that?"

He nodded. "Yeah. We're good. In fact, if you want to stay up there and eat, you go ahead."

"Okay." She pivoted and all but ran to the front door.

He scrubbed his hand down his face. If he really wanted to keep himself in line around the nanny, he didn't need to formulate a plan for the place of women in his life. All he had to do was remember how badly his last relationship had turned out. The pain of realizing he'd been used. The pain of discovering Liliah wanted nothing to do with his babies. She had been a boatload of trouble and drama.

He frowned. Liliah *had been* a boatload of drama and trouble. And that was probably why Tory was so attractive to him. She was Liliah's polar opposite. Nice, sweet and kind to his babies, Tory didn't bring an ounce of drama to his life.

But, after Liliah, even if Tory were his soul mate, a relationship wasn't worth risking his trouble-free, drama-free household. And being involved with the nanny would certainly bring drama.

He'd had his share of drama with Liliah.

He didn't want any more. No matter what form it took.

The next morning, Tory carried both babies into the kitchen. She slid them into their highchairs and began mixing cereal. "So, I take it everybody slept well."

Cindy giggled and Sam yelped.

"Hey, hey, Sammy! I get it. You're hungry. And I'm hurrying. But there's only one of me. So you have to be patient."

She took the two bowls of cereal to the table, pulled out a chair and arranged it between both highchairs. "Okay. It's just us now. So everybody has to be on best behavior."

Sam squealed, slapping his hands on the highchair tray.

"Did you not hear the part about best behavior? Your dad is exhausted and we're letting him sleep in."

She spooned a helping of cereal into Sam's mouth. He smacked his lips in innocent enjoyment.

She laughed, wanting to pinch his chubby little cheek. Instead, she fed Cindy a spoon of cereal. "But I'm also sort of trying to butter him up. We never talked about days off and we have to because—"

She paused, cleared her throat, not sure why she couldn't quite bring herself to talk about Jason with two babies who probably wouldn't understand a word she said.

Except that the situation with Jason was sad and they were happy. Sam was a chubby, giggly little guy and Cindy was petite, demure. Probably someday she'd be exactly like Gwen. It seemed wrong to tell them about something so tragic when they were so cheerful.

So she wouldn't tell them, but she had to tell Chance. She had to ask for days off.

Chance stretched lazily when he woke. His back didn't hurt. His head was clear. And his muscles felt great. He was almost energetic.

He bounced up in bed and his gaze flew to the clock. It was almost nine!

The kids!

Why weren't they screaming?

He rolled to get out from under the thin sheet that covered him and saw the blue drapes on the big window.

Not his house. His mom's guesthouse.

And he hadn't gotten up with the kids in the middle of the night because they now had a nanny.

A godsend nanny.

Well, the woman who would be a godsend if she weren't so damned good-looking.

He passed his hand down his face, reminded himself that Tory was a drama-free employee whom he wanted to keep and headed for the bathroom. He didn't hear any crying and he also had a meeting that morning, so he stepped into the shower in his private bathroom and scrubbed himself off.

Alone.

No kids sitting in front of the glass shower door, in the little basket-like seats Liliah had dropped them off in, crying as he took one of the shortest showers in recorded history.

For this and this alone, he could keep his hormones under control around the nanny. Because the other thing he'd figured out—before he drifted off to sleep the night before—was that *she* wasn't the problem. *She* hadn't done anything wrong. In fact, she'd more or less told him she wasn't interested in him by her behavior at the discount department store. Which meant anything he'd taken to be attraction on her part, *he'd* misinterpreted.

So he was the one who had to get in line. And that should be a piece of cake. He'd been ignoring women for fifteen months now.

He dressed in trousers and a white shirt and tie and walked through the great room into the kitchen area. Tory had the babies in the two highchairs, and was alternating feeding them. Her auburn hair had been caught up in a long ponytail that made her look about twenty, but she wore baggy jeans and a blousy top that hid all of her curves.

Still, when he saw her, his stomach jumped. Nerve endings he didn't even know he had bounced to attention.

She smiled at him. "Hey, good morning." Her gaze tumbled from his head to his toes and her smile grew. "Well, look at you."

His mouth went dry. He tried to say good morning, but when the words came out they were more like a jumble of mush.

"I have coffee."

"Great." He walked to the pot, scolding himself for being ridiculous. Yes, she was pretty. And, yes, it had been a long time since he'd really looked at a woman—and since one had looked at him. But she was dressed in clothes obviously not meant to attract him. So the once-over she'd given him was nothing more than a friendly acknowledgment that he looked better in a shirt and tie than blue jeans.

He had to stop reacting to her. He needed her.

As a nanny.

He found a mug, poured himself some coffee

and took a swallow before he said, "Are you okay being alone with the kids this morning?"

She smiled at him. A big, beaming smile that made her brown eyes sparkle. "That's sort of my job."

His hormones jumped again. Every fiber of his being wanted to flirt with her. But, again, she might be friendly, but she wasn't flirting. Any attraction he thought he saw was strictly in his head or maybe wishful thinking.

He sucked in a breath. "Great. Because I actually have a meeting with my brother."

"Ah. That explains the tie."

He flapped it away from his shirt, and let it fall down again. "Dead giveaway, huh?"

"Well, I didn't think you'd need one to go to your mom's for breakfast."

He caught her gaze. "She doesn't require a tie for breakfast, but she does for dinner."

Tory winced. "Sounds fun."

"It's a pain in the butt. Just like this meeting with my brother is going to be." He finished his coffee, walked back into his room and grabbed his suit jacket.

Striding through the great room to the front

door, he said, "I don't expect to be back for a few hours—probably two."

"Okay." She turned to Cindy and Sam. "Say goodbye to your daddy, kids."

Both kids squawked happily.

He groaned in his head. She had him so tripped up that he'd forgotten to say goodbye to his own kids.

After a quick kiss to the top of each twin's head, he left the cottage and jumped into his SUV, blowing his breath out on a long sigh. He told himself to think of Liliah, to remember relationships were always trouble. To remember he didn't want to be hurt. To remember he didn't want his kids to be hurt by another woman who abandoned them.

He started the SUV and headed up the lane to the street. Twenty minutes later, he stood outside the yellow brick Montgomery Development building. Quiet and dignified, it sat among buildings older and taller and yet it still somehow intimidated him. How could four measly stories project such an air of power?

He sucked in a breath. It was no wonder he was tired of drama. Not only had Liliah made him miserable, but with the exception of Gwen, his family life had been trouble too. He'd thought all that was over when his dad died, but his brother had relentlessly followed him for the past few years, trying to get him to come home. He'd always managed to give him the slip, until last week when he couldn't take the babies and run.

So after Max called, he'd called their mom to talk things through with her, and he'd come home. Not to placate his brother and certainly not forever. He would always call Gwen Mom, and now that the truth was out about his dad, he would always have a relationship with her. But he wasn't sure he wanted a relationship with the brother who'd kept their dad's secret. And he had a feeling the only way to stay away from persistent Max would be to go back to Tennessee.

Blowing his breath out on a long sigh, he headed for the entryway. He would let his brother have his say, thank him for any offers he made and refuse them. He wouldn't start trouble. He wouldn't open old wounds. There didn't need to be any arguments. He would calmly ask his brother to let him alone—for good this time—and be done with this.

He stepped through the glass double doors and stopped, totally surprised. Vaulted ceilings soared to the roof. Sunshine poured in through skylights and fed the potted trees that sat on each side of the two white sofas in the reception area. A polished yellow wood reception desk sat in the center of everything.

Wow. His mom had said Max had changed things, but he hadn't expected that would mean even the building.

Dark brown travertine tile led him to the reception desk. The pretty twentysomething brunette greeted him with a smile. "Can I help you?"

"Yes. I have an appointment with Mr. Montgomery."

She glanced down at a small computer screen. "Your name?"

"Chance." He paused. "Montgomery."

The young woman glanced up at him with a raised eyebrow. He scowled at her. If Max thought he would jump through hoops to get to see him, he was sadly mistaken.

"If it's that much of a bother to see my big brother, even with an appointment, I'll just go."

The receptionist held up a hand to stop him.

"No. No problem! I'm sorry. Just give me a second to announce you." She pressed two buttons on her phone then turned away.

He heard the receptionist say his name, then give his description.

Then there was silence.

Annoyance flooded him. This was what he'd hated about being a Montgomery. The pretense. As if he were the king of England, Max screened his visitors.

The receptionist faced him. "I'm sorry, Mr. Montgomery. You may go up."

"Gee, thanks."

Obviously recognizing how insulted he was, the receptionist grimaced. "Take the third elevator in the back of that hall." She pointed to the left. "By the time you get there, a security guard will be there to punch in the code."

He ambled to the last elevator, the temptation to leave tickling his brain. He'd told Max he wanted no part of this pomp and circumstance, yet the first thing he did was run him through a lineup.

Before he knew it, he was at the elevator. The security guard said, "Good morning, Mr. Montgomery." Punching a few numbers into a keypad, he opened the elevator, motioned Chance inside and stepped back as the doors closed.

The ride to the fourth floor took seconds. The elevator doors swooshed open. More potted trees accented a low, ultramodern green sofa and chair. A green print rug covered part of the yellow hardwood floor.

Sitting at the desk in front of a wall of windows, Max looked up and instantly rose.

When they were kids, everyone would comment on how cute it was that they both had dark hair and blue eyes, even though Chance had been adopted. Now, everyone knew why.

"Chance. Sorry about that mess up downstairs. I told them you were coming. I also told them to give you the code for the elevator."

He flopped on the sofa before Max invited him to sit down. "Well, they didn't."

"And you're mad."

"No, actually, they made my case about why I don't want to work here. Dad would be so proud."

"Dad had nothing to do with just about everything that goes on here now. I changed how we do business with subcontractors and vendors. We don't make backdoor deals with unions. We don't cheat employees out of bonuses. And I won't lock you out of a company that's as much yours as mine."

Chance said, "*Humph.* Mom said you were different."

Max sat on the chair across from him. "Losing your wife, admitting you're an alcoholic and going to AA will do that to you."

Chance sat up. The alcoholic thing floored him, but Kate leaving shocked him so much he forgot he was angry. Though Max and Kate were older, the trio had been like the Three Musketeers before he ran away. Chance had loved Kate like a sister. "You and Kate split up?"

"For eight years. She kept my daughter, Trisha, from me. She just left and didn't even tell me she was pregnant."

"Holy cow."

"It took a while, but we reconciled."

"And the alcoholic thing? Was that because she left?"

Max shook his head. "I became an alcoholic after *you* left, Chance."

He froze. "Me?"

"I loved you, kid. Still do. You're my brother.

I was sorry for everything that happened and I shouldered all the responsibility and the blame. And started drinking. But after Kate left, I realized drinking wasn't helping and once I got sober, I saw how bad Dad really was. I learned every department, read every lease, talked to every contractor and vendor. And ultimately took over."

Chance gaped at him. "You kicked Dad out?"

"He resigned—sort of happily, really. His last two years he and Mom traveled." He shrugged. "I'm not just blowing smoke when I say things have changed. The company is different. I am different. You can trust me." He rose from his seat. "Rather than talk about what I've done, let me give you a tour of the place." He motioned to a richly detailed, double-door entrance. "And you can see for yourself how different the company is and see for yourself that I'm not running it like Dad."

Chance also rose, but he rose slowly, without any enthusiasm. He might have a strange sympathy for his brother rattling through him now, but that didn't mean he wanted to work for him. "I don't know, Max."

"Come on. What can it hurt to look?"

He shook his head. "I don't want to. I've distanced myself from you and the company."

"And you hate me?"

"No more than you hate me."

Max frowned. "Why would I hate you?"

"Because you grew up as the favorite son. The 'real' Montgomery child, while I was adopted. Then we all found out I'm as much of a Montgomery as you are. That had to sting."

"Not really." He sighed. "Look. I don't think we hate each other. I think we had one ugly family fight. I'm not going to let that stand in the way of our being a family. Mom wants this."

A warm feeling flowed through him at the mention of their mom, the woman who loved him even though he was the product of her husband's affair. So did the reminder that in some respects he owed her.

Max turned him in the direction of his office door. "I'm not going to browbeat you into coming to work for me. We can give Mom a family without you working for me. Hell, you can move back to Tennessee and we can still be a family.

But if you like what you see, why wouldn't you want to work here?"

Chance laughed. "Because I have my own company?"

"Who's running it while you're away?"

"I have a manager."

"Who I am sure would be happy to continue running it." Max slapped him on the back. "Wait until you see what we're doing, little brother. You're going to want to be part of this."

CHAPTER THREE

SOMETIME AFTER TWO, Chance rushed into the cottage as if late for his own wedding. Tory wasn't sure if that was a good sign or a bad sign, but it didn't matter. When he'd come out of his bedroom that morning, she hadn't talked to him about days off because he seemed so nervous. But whether it was convenient or not, she had to talk to him now—tell him about Jason—so she could at least visit him two days a week.

Bouncing chubby Sam on her hip, she said, "Whoa! Where's the fire?"

"I'm so sorry for leaving you with them for so long! I didn't expect to stay with my brother all morning." He shook his head as if confused. "I didn't expect to talk more than twenty minutes let alone have lunch with him. I'm so sorry."

She pointed at her chest. "Nanny." Pointed at him. "Boss. You call the shots. It's my job to stay with the kids while you do anything you have to do." She kissed the top of Sam's head. "Besides, they're so adorable. It's hardly a job to stay with them. More like playing."

"That's because they're good when they're with you." He tossed his keys to the table behind the sofa. "I'm seeing a whole new side of them around you." Leaning down he plucked Cindy from the play yard. Kissed her cheek. "How's Daddy's good girl today?"

She cooed a laugh. He kissed her again.

And Tory's heart swelled. In the years she'd been undergoing surgeries and therapies, she hadn't really thought about kids. She hadn't thought about anything but visiting Jason and repairing her own damaged leg. But suddenly these two—feisty Sam and sweet Cindy—brought out longings in her that she couldn't deny. And she was so afraid she was about to jeopardize being in their lives by asking for time off. But she also had responsibilities to Jason.

"So do you want to go up to the house for your lunch? I apologize that it's so late. You're probably starving."

She ambled toward the sofa. "Actually, Cook

had Robert make a delivery today. But I would like to talk to you about something."

A panicked expression flitted across his face. "Okay."

She motioned to one of the two chairs near the sofa. "Don't worry. It's not really a bad thing."

He sat, arranging Cindy on his lap. "Why don't you let me be the judge of that?"

"I just need a day or two off every week."

He looked at her. "That's it?"

"Well, I've never been a nanny before, but it seems to be a twenty-four/seven job. And I need two days off because I usually—" She cleared her throat. "It's just that I have to—" She paused, once again floundering about how to explain her situation. She didn't want his pity. She also felt odd sharing something so personal with a man she barely knew and she couldn't do it.

"There's someplace I like to go twice a week."

His eyebrows rose. "Oh?"

She settled Sam on her lap and he happily gurgled up at her. "Just a girl thing."

He studied her face for a few seconds, then said, "Honestly, Tory, I've never employed a nanny and I don't remember the nanny my mom says cared for me, but I do know that everybody's entitled to a day off every now and again. So if you want two days, you just tell me which two days and I'll make do."

"I hate to ask because I know this job is only temporary. A few days or weeks—"

Cindy started to fuss and Chance said, "Hold that thought," as he rose from his chair. "How long has it been since their last bottle?"

She rose too. "Actually, it's nap time."

He turned. "It is?"

"Yes. I decided this morning that we should try to put them on a schedule." She winced. "I probably should have run that by you."

"No. That's fine. You know more about babies than I do. I want you to change whatever needs changing."

"Good." She headed for the kitchen, got two bottles and followed him into the nursery.

"They're drinking them cold?"

"I tested that this morning too. They didn't seem to mind cold milk. It saves a step in all the processes. Plus, it makes it easier if you're somewhere that you can't heat the bottles."

"Okay."

They sat on the rockers in the nursery and fed the babies enough milk to put them to sleep, then gently laid them down for their naps and tiptoed out of the nursery.

For the first time since their little argument the day before, she and Chance were alone. Unsure of what to do, she stopped on the edge of the great room, the big open space that basically included the kitchen, the TV area and even the little reading cove. The only place to "hide" was her room. Or she could go outside. But they hadn't finished their conversation about her days off.

He ambled into the kitchen. "Do we have any soda?"

"I think that's the one thing your mom forgot to stock."

"I'll call Cook." Retrieving a bottle of juice, he stepped away from the refrigerator. "She's the shopper for both houses."

She smiled. "That's good." She supposed. Her parents were blue-collar. She'd never run a home. She had no clue how the house of a rich family ran. God, suddenly she felt incredibly inadequate, unworldly.

He popped the top on the juice and plopped

down on the recliner. In a white shirt, with the sleeves rolled to the elbows, he looked sexily rumpled, the way a husband would when he came home to his wife.

Oh, boy. Where had that come from?

But she knew where it came from. She was attracted to him. Not just because he was good-looking but because he was the daddy of babies she adored. That was wrong on so many levels, she wanted to run, but knew she couldn't. Not only did she have to get adjusted to living with him, but also she had to get her days off locked in so she could go and see her *fiancé*. And then maybe she'd stop looking at Chance as if she were allowed.

"So two days off will be good?"

He chugged half his bottle of juice, then said, "You pick the days."

"Okay. Give me some time to think about which days I want and I'll let you know."

"Good."

"Good."

The room got quiet again.

She glanced around.

Now what? She wanted to run again, but really, she would be living with this guy for at least two weeks. Maybe even a month. If she didn't get herself accustomed to being in his company, she'd always be slightly on edge around him, like a silly schoolgirl. It seemed wise to try to get them both accustomed to being around each other. And if a little conversation would do it, then she'd converse.

She cleared her throat. "So how'd things go with your brother?"

"Same old. Same old. He wants me to come work for Montgomery Development."

Relief skittered through her. He hadn't thought it odd she'd asked him a question, and she really was interested in what was going on with him. Had to be. What went on in his life affected what went on in hers.

She inched her way over to the sofa. "You don't want to work for Montgomery Development?"

"I already own my own company, remember? I don't need a job."

She stifled the urge to gape at him. What would that be like? To be so lucky in life that you didn't need a job? She slid a little closer to the couch.

"You said you have a manager running your company now."

"Uh-huh. Max thinks I should just let him keep running it so I could help him with Montgomery Development." He winced. "As president."

She fell to the sofa. That went beyond lucky. "President?"

"He's CEO and Chairman of the Board. Technically, he'd still be my boss."

"Wow."

"It is a great company." His face grew thoughtful. "It was a crappy company when I left. My dad was a scoundrel. He nickel and dimed everybody. Out-and-out cheated others." He snorted a laugh. "I wouldn't have worked there on a lost bet while he was alive, but in the past years my brother changed things. The company's more than reputable. And growing. Some of the things Max is into are mind-boggling. I think I'd like to be part of that."

She frowned. "So you'd stay?"

He grimaced. "I think I'm talking myself into it. I know my mother wants me to stay. I know she wants to be part of the twins' lives. And I hurt her enough by leaving when I was eighteen and staying away that I feel I owe her that."

"That's very nice."

He shrugged and wouldn't look at her. "But that means the nanny job could be yours permanently…if you want it."

Her breath caught. It was only her second day of work, but she already liked it here. She had the run of the house when he was away, and if he worked he'd be away all day. And she had two adorable babies to play with to fill the aching hole in her heart that she didn't even realize she had until she held them.

And Chance himself was kinda nice. Easy to talk to. For years, she hadn't spoken with anyone beyond therapists and nurses and her parents—and Jason, who didn't reply.

The only problem was her attraction—but surely she could keep that under control. After all, she had a fiancé. A fiancé she'd visit twice a week, now that Chance had agreed to two days off.

She licked her lips. "It would mean I'd have to take my days off on Saturdays or Sundays."

He caught her gaze. "Or I could work something out with my mom."

"You don't have to accommodate me."

"I like you."

Her heart stumbled in her chest. With their gazes locked and the sounds of chirping birds in the backyard, she felt a million things at once, but the biggest one was happiness. She told herself that was because she liked this job, but staring into his blue eyes, she knew that wasn't entirely true. She liked *him*. He was interesting and funny and appreciative of her help. He made her feel needed, useful. And pretty. He didn't even have to say the words. She could see it in the way he looked at her.

"And I want to keep you as a nanny."

"Of course." Idiot. Did she think he liked her romantically after thirty-six hours? And what was she doing spinning fantasies? Hadn't she said she could handle this attraction? Yes. She had. Because she could. Because being attracted to him was wrong. And she wasn't stupid. "But I want to be fair too."

He rose from his seat. "Why don't we just give it a trial run and see how it goes? See if Saturdays and Sundays are good days off for you or see if we need to make other arrangements."

He smiled at her, and that thing in her heart tripped again. This time it made her blood rush through her veins and her head feel light.

"Don't forget my mom has a whole staff we can call upon for help when you need time off."

So confused she couldn't speak, she nodded.

"But right now, if you don't mind, I'd like to get out of these clothes and maybe take a short walk around the grounds before the kids get up from their naps."

"That'd be great. I mean—fine. It's my job to be here."

He laughed and left the room, but Tory collapsed on the sofa. What the hell was wrong with her? Yes, he was good-looking. But he was out of her league. And *her boss*! He didn't like her and even if he did, she couldn't like him. She was committed to Jason.

The little slip about liking her had been the result of testosterone bubbling around again, so Chance had decided to leave the house to cool off. But he hadn't gotten three feet into the woods before his head cleared, he began thinking logically again and he stopped dead in his tracks.

She had a secret.

That's why she'd stumbled over her explanation for wanting days off. That's why she wouldn't exactly say where she would be going on those days. There was something about her life she didn't want to tell him.

Not that she couldn't keep her personal life private, but…

His life had been built on secrets and lies. After his dad and Liliah, he really needed honesty from the people in his life. Max had won back a lot of Chance's trust that morning with simple language and truth rather than doublespeak, but now his otherwise perfect nanny was holding something back.

Still, that might actually be good, depending on her secret. She had a right to a private life and her secret probably pertained to something that wasn't connected to him or the twins. But, more important, being as picky as he was about trust, finding out she was hiding something totally turned him off. So he didn't have to worry about his runaway feelings for her anymore. They were gone.

That was the good part.

The bad part was the secret itself. Did he really want to leave his kids with someone who was keeping something from him?

With that in mind, he cut his walk short. He heard the kids fussing as he entered, and immediately went back to the nursery to find Tory changing Cindy while Sam cried in his crib. He changed Sam's diaper and he and Tory played with the twins a bit before she walked to the mansion to have her supper.

Not only had his attraction suspended, but she hadn't seemed nervous or upset in the time they spent together, so he decided her secret had to be personal. Something like a boyfriend she met twice a week.

Which was good. Let her have a secret love. All the better to help him keep his distance from her.

When she returned, Chance had the babies on the floor, letting them try to crawl.

Tory raced over and stooped down in front of them. "Well, look at you! Learning to crawl!" She clapped her hands together with glee and

Chance smiled at her, but just as quickly as his lips quirked upward, they fell again.

She has a boyfriend. His stomach tightened as disappointment rumbled through him. If her secret was anything else—a bad job recommendation, a firing, a felony—something would have shown up when his mom checked her references before she hired her.

He tried to tell himself that he'd met lots of already-taken women in his lifetime and walked away from all of them as naturally as breathing, but that didn't make the regret go away.

Why did having to keep his distance from this woman bother him?

"How about a snack and then bath time," she said, taking Cindy with her as she rose from the floor.

"Sounds good." He rose too, reminding himself she had a right to a private life—and a boyfriend—and he had to get over himself.

They fed the kids a bit of cereal and headed for the nursery bathroom. Because his mom had done her best to accommodate twins, there were two sinks in the counter.

"Too bad they're too big to fit in these sinks."

Carrying Cindy on her hip, Tory brought two plastic baby tubs over from the bathroom closet. "Yeah, but your mom did think of these."

He pulled them apart, used the hose apparatus to fill them and then undressed Sam.

Loving the water, Sam slapped it with his chubby hands.

Nodding at him, Tory said, "Pretty soon he's not going to fit that tub."

Chance laughed. "No. He's not."

"Then we'll have to use the big bathtub."

"Is that dangerous?"

"Not if we never leave him." She smiled at Chance. "Childcare is a matter of a little bit of knowledge and lots of common sense."

He remembered all the things she'd already taught him. In a little less than two days, his kids were happy and he felt more competent.

Wistfulness stole through him. Even with a boyfriend, she could still be an excellent nanny, but they'd lost something. He wanted to like her. She was sweet and funny. The kind of woman he needed after Liliah.

Liliah. Just thinking her name caused anger to spiral through him. It reminded him of the humiliation he'd felt after she'd admitted she'd only dated him to use him. He'd known her weeks before they'd gotten romantically involved, and still she'd fooled him. Wasn't it a tad stupid to be so quickly falling for Tory? A woman he really didn't know? A woman with a secret? Probably a boyfriend.

God. Where was his brain around her?

Tory squeezed a washcloth full of water over Cindy's head. Streams ran through her curls and made her giggle.

That's where his brain was. On his kids. Tory was so good with his kids and his kids were so needy that he was taking his feelings of appreciation too far. Maybe he wanted a mother for his kids so badly that he was seeing things in her that weren't really there.

Well, no more.

"And little miss Cindy likes her bath too."

She eased the cloth over Cindy's soft belly as Chance washed Sam. They rolled the two wet, squirming babies into fat, fluffy towels and headed to the nursery where they slid them into one-piece pajamas. They fed them bottles, let them drift off to sleep and then left the nursery.

Alone in the great room again, Chance had himself totally under control. He ambled into the sitting area, snagging the remote for the TV from the coffee table and fell to the sofa.

Right beside Tory.

Assuming she'd gone to her room, he hadn't even looked before sitting, and suddenly they were hip to hip, virtually on top of each other.

His gaze snapped to hers. An apology sprang to his lips. But her brown eyes heated with such yearning that he stopped it.

Warmth spiraled through him. With one simple reach of his hand, he could slide his fingers under her luxurious auburn hair, bring her face to his and press his lips to hers.

Satisfy this hunger that snaked through him every time he looked at her.

As if reading his thoughts, she sucked in a breath. Her breasts rose and fell and sweet need sprang up again.

Then he remembered Liliah. He remembered the humiliation of realizing he'd totally misjudged her and the anger when she abandoned their kids. He remembered he barely knew Tory and that she had a secret.

He bounced from the sofa. “You know what? I’m more tired than I thought.” He pivoted and headed for his bedroom. “I think I’ll just call it a night.”

CHAPTER FOUR

THE SOUND OF THE BABIES crying woke Tory a little after three and she popped up in bed. Shoving her arms into her pink chenille robe to the music of two wailing babies, she limped to the nursery door. Her leg always bothered her after hours of sitting or when she first awoke, so it didn't concern her. She opened the door from her room to the nursery just as Chance opened the door on the other side, the one that connected to his room.

His short dark hair spiked out in all directions. His eyes blinked against the light she'd turned on. And he was topless. He wore only black sweatpants that hung low on his lean hips, revealing a firm chest peppered with hair as black as the hair on his head. Even his feet were bare.

Her breathing froze. Their moment on the couch rolled through her brain. The shivery heat that had rattled through her flooded her again. She'd never felt anything like that for a man before. Not even Jason. Which made it incredibly wrong. Incredibly. It had to be.

She quickly headed for Cindy's crib. "I thought it was my job to get up with the babies?"

The question stuttered out of her, but she had to say something. Not only did she need to get them past the ridiculous once-over she'd just given his body, but she also wanted to get them beyond her gazing at him like a lovesick fool while they were on the sofa. He might be gorgeous, with a fantastic, sexy, sensual body. But that wasn't his fault. It was nature's. After the way she'd stared longingly at him when they'd accidentally sat side by side on the sofa, she had to show him she could behave appropriately around him. Like a nanny.

He ran his hand down his face. "A full night's sleep last night was wonderful. But there are two of them and two of us. It will just make things easier if we work together."

His deep, masculine voice set off a chain reaction of tingles and fluttering inside her. She wanted to ask herself what was wrong with her but she knew. Just as nature had graced Chance with good looks, it was interfering with her biology now. She was a normal twenty-five-year-old woman. Her hormones might have been suppressed for the years she'd gone through surgeries and rehab but they were awake now.

Still, she could ignore them. She *had to* ignore them.

They made short order of the diapers in silence. When the last snap was snapped, Chance walked over to Cindy's changing table and motioned for Tory to put her on his free arm.

"Since I can hold both, you get the bottles."

She slid the baby onto his arm, taking great care not to touch him. Then she scooted out and raced to the kitchen. She took two bottles from the refrigerator, and headed back to the nursery. Nudging open the door with her shoulder, she found Chance struggling with his two screaming bundles of joy, both of whom appeared to want to crawl onto his head.

She raced over with the bottles, simultaneously handing Chance a bottle and taking Cindy from his lap. "I see what you mean about them crawling all over you like cats."

Sliding the nipple into Sam's mouth, Chance only grunted. She sat on the other rocker and slid the bottle into Cindy's mouth.

Except for the eager sucking of two hungry babies, the room was silent.

Tory drew in a long breath. They shouldn't talk. The kids should eat and then fall back to sleep. But not talking made the time seem so intimate.

She snorted a laugh in her head. The intimacy was only her perception. A guy who jumped off the couch and ran to his room rather than sit too close to her and grunted his responses wasn't feeling intimate. She had to get ahold of these weird feelings and stop misinterpreting things. He was her boss. She was a nanny. He needed her. And she liked being needed. She liked being around the kids.

Sam finished first. Chance expertly burped him and put him in his crib with a soft good-night kiss. Without a word, he left the nursery, confirming that all these things she thought were happening were only in her head.

Sleepy Cindy sucked slowly and drifted off to sleep.

"Hey," Tory whispered. "You can't fall asleep until you're done eating."

Cindy blinked up at her as if saying her talking

helped her to stay awake, so Tory smiled. "You like a little dinner conversation?"

Cindy kept her eyes on Tory's.

"Such a pretty girl," she whispered, stroking Cindy's forehead as the baby suckled. "I think we're going to have to teach your daddy to talk a bit when he feeds you."

Cindy's eyes closed again and Tory glanced down at the bottle. It was empty. She woke Cindy long enough to get her to burp, then laid her in the crib.

Standing at the door, with her hand poised over the light, she suddenly wished Chance would take the job with his family's company and keep her as a nanny. Then she could watch these kids grow up.

That was foolish dreaming. Dangerous dreaming.

Or was it? The doctors had said they had no idea how long Jason would be in his coma. And she had no intention of deserting him. Being a nanny for the next eighteen years gave her something she wouldn't otherwise get—a chance to be a mom.

Was it so wrong to want that?

It served everybody's purposes. Chance got the help he needed raising his children. She got to be a mom of sorts, even though she'd never marry.

It seemed perfect.

Except for her damned attraction.

No. She couldn't stay here forever. Six years tops. Which gave her enough time to finish her degree at nights—if she buckled down.

Maybe she should start thinking about that and not daydreaming about kids who weren't hers.

The next morning Chance had another appointment with his brother. He dressed in a suit and tie again and all but raced out of the house—except this time he remembered to kiss the kids.

But when he was alone in the SUV, their "almost" minute on the sofa the night before jumped into his head. He had to fight the urge not to bang his head against the steering wheel. How could he even think about kissing Tory with Liliah's antics so fresh in his brain? Especially since Tory had "somewhere" to go on Saturdays and Sundays. She might not have a boyfriend, but she had a secret.

He sucked in a breath. A secret that probably wasn't any of his business. Tory was an employee. And maybe if he started thinking of her *only* as an employee some of these "other" feelings would go away.

He shoved the car key in the ignition. "What she does on her own time is none of my business."

Except the most reasonable, most innocent explanation had been ruled out when they'd met in the nursery for the twins' middle-of-the-night feeding and she'd stared at him as if she hadn't seen a man in years.

Plus, she'd stuttered over the reason why she wanted time off. She'd groped for a way not to have to tell him where she was going and in the end settled on just being vague. And if his relationship with Liliah had taught him anything, it was to be suspicious of people who were deliberately vague.

So his shields were back up. He'd think of her only as an employee and even then he'd be careful. He would not—absolutely would not—tolerate any more drama in his life. And if this secret of hers brought any, he was going to fire her.

Period.

Reasoning that through should have made him happy, but it actually made him antsy. Angry, but with a nervous twist. He didn't want to fire her. He didn't want her to have a secret. He didn't want to have to fight his attraction. He wanted to be able to pursue it.

Which annoyed the hell out of him.

What was it about this woman that he couldn't stop thinking about her, even when common sense told him something was wrong?

He pulled into the executive parking lot for Montgomery Development, got out of his SUV and used the private elevator to go to Max's office. When the elevator doors opened, the sofa and chairs were filled to capacity with men and women in gray, black and navy blue suits.

Relief poured through him. Business. This was his domain. This would get his mind off Tory and her secrets and her soft brown eyes.

He stepped into the office and like a proud big brother, Max said, "Everyone, this is my brother Chance."

As Max recited names, Chance shook a long row of hands, suddenly feeling a part of things. He knew that was because Max introduced him as if it were a foregone conclusion that he'd be staying in Pine Ward. But as the day wore on, Max's behavior began to strike him as being odd as the nanny's.

Why was he going to such great lengths to be nice? To include him? The big brother he'd left hadn't so much been bad as he'd been an attention grabber. Knowing he'd be taking over Montgomery Development, Max had all but shadowed their dad, wanting to be just like him. Now, suddenly, he was different? How had Max bamboozled him into believing that?

Antsy as he was, Chance couldn't let this slide. In fact, antsy as he was, he was sort of looking forward to a fight.

When the day was done, he took the seat in front of Max's desk, and Max walked to the tall-back chair behind it. "So what did you think? Does Montgomery Development look like the place you could work for the next twenty or so years?"

Chance smiled wryly. Without even realizing it, his brother was handing him his argument opportunity on a silver platter. He snorted a laugh. "Right to the point, huh?"

"Hey, I don't know how long you're going to be here. I have to get to the point."

"All right. You want to know what I think? I think you're going to make promises like Dad did then back out of them once you have me here."

Max gaped at him. "Have the past two days meant nothing to you?"

"You were a charmer just like Dad, Max. And I'm supposed to believe you've changed?"

Max's chair creaked as he leaned back. "Go on."

"Go on? I'd rather just go before you cheat me or lie to me or withhold important information."

"Oh." Max snorted a laugh. "I get what you're doing. You *want* me to be just like Dad. You *want* to make me the bad guy so you can tell Mom you tried, but I'm impossible to work with." He stood, leaned across the desk. "Get this, little brother. You own one-third of this company. When Mom passes, we'll each own half. We are stuck with each other. And I don't want to do all the work myself. I want some help. So let's just have this out right now."

Chance rose too, leaned across the desk as Max had done. "Fine. You want to have it out? Let's start with why you didn't tell me you knew Dad was my biological father?"

Max leaned closer. "Because I'd only heard office gossip. I wasn't about to take gossip to you. Now I get a question. If you're such a great guy who loves Mom so much, why didn't you at least send a Christmas card in fifteen years?"

"I was angry."

"Well, la-di-da."

Just seeing his big, bad brother say, "La-di-da," sent Chance's lips to twitching. In a few seconds, he was laughing. "La-di-da?"

Max fell to his seat. "Seemed appropriate at the time."

Chance laughed again.

Max motioned to his chair. "So you're afraid to work with me?"

Chance sat. If this was his moment of truth with his brother, then it was going to be a genuine moment of truth. No hedging. No accusations. Just the truth. Because as much as he wanted to, he couldn't work here. "I can't trust you, Max."

"All because I knew something for twenty-four hours without telling you?"

"I don't know. Maybe. But it's more about Dad.

About connections to this place that I can't seem to shake. I spent fifteen years disliking you. That just doesn't go away."

"Fair enough."

He glanced up sharply. "Fair enough?"

"I think you're asking for time. I'm happy to give it to you."

"I just told you I don't trust you and you're telling me that you'll give me time?"

"Time to come to terms with everything. Time to trust me." He leaned his chair back again. "Chance, I'm an alcoholic who had to make amends to at least half the people in town. I've had to be patient while nearly everyone I knew got adjusted to the new me. I'd be a real idiot if I couldn't wait for my own brother to adjust."

Chance said nothing. He'd never heard such sincerity come from anyone. And if there was anyone he longed to give a second chance, it was Max. The older brother he'd at one time adored.

Max steepled his fingers and tapped them against his mouth for a few seconds before he opened the top drawer of his desk. "Since we're being honest and up front and open and all that great stuff—" he tossed a manila envelope at him "—this is yours."

Chance didn't even reach for the envelope. "What is it?"

"Open it."

He lifted the envelope, opened it and pulled out a stack of at least five annual statements for Montgomery Development.

"You want me to see how well the company's done or the history of what you've changed since Dad died?"

"I've been catching you up the past few days. Those annual statements are for you to check numbers."

"Check numbers?"

"Reach a little farther into the envelope."

He did and found a bankbook.

"That's your share of our profits since Dad died. After he passed, Mom decided that she didn't need or want all the money Montgomery Development generated, so she made us full partners. As I said, we each own a third. That—" he nodded at the bankbook "—is your share."

He opened the bankbook. Glanced up at Max. "There are millions of dollars here."

"I know."

"You left it in a savings account? Where it barely draws interest?"

Max laughed. "My job was to keep your money safe. Your job is to invest it."

"I don't know what to say." He really didn't. Their father would have never held profits. Not even for a partner. He would have figured a way take them as salary or a bonus. Max had saved them. For him.

"Say you'll stay…at least a while. Give me a chance to prove myself. Things are very different here now. We could be a family again."

A family. The real gift he wanted to give the twins. An uncle, an aunt, cousins, a grandma. And Max wanted it too. Yet, here he was, picking a fight because he couldn't trust.

He cleared his throat and unexpectedly thought of Tory. Like Max, she'd been nothing but good to him, and what did he do? Convince himself he couldn't trust her because of Liliah, and build a federal case out of her not telling him where she would be going on her days off.

He swallowed hard. "What if the problem isn't

that I don't trust you but that I just plain can't trust at all?"

"Then I would recommend that you stay even more. You build trust first with family, Chance. Give me and Mom the opportunity to show you that we love you and we want you in our lives. And we'll take it from there."

He laughed slightly and shook his head, realizing what a yutz he'd been. "You mean start interacting more than just living in Mom's guesthouse and visiting you on the job?"

"Yeah. You can't write off me and Mom because Dad was a jerk. Get to know us before you write us off."

Max's words rang in Chance's head as he entered the cottage that night. Because it was already after six, Tory had the babies fed.

"That was a long visit."

"My brother and I had a talk—"

And he had been so confused about his mistrust of Tory—whether it was leftover feelings from Liliah or genuine mistrust because she had a secret—that he didn't really want to come home. So he'd driven around a bit, trying to make sense of what was happening. He didn't want to fall victim to an unexpectedly intense attraction. Yet he didn't want to lose a good nanny because he said or did something because of his overly suspicious mind. He did want to do what Max had suggested, get to know the new people around him. But the problem was, getting to know Tory usually either made him giddy with attraction or suspicious of her.

He had to find a neutral ground and had no idea how.

He walked over to the play yard, and lifted Sam out. "Hey, big guy. What did you do all day?"

"Actually, they had a special day."

He peered over. "They did?"

"Yes, your mom has decided to keep them every day at noon while I eat lunch."

He laughed, felt some of his apprehension loosen. This was a normal discussion a man should have with his children's nanny. If he could keep the conversation going like this, he might actually get comfortable. "I knew she wouldn't be able to resist."

"She is their grandmother."

"Technically, yes."

"Technically?"

Maybe it was time for him to be a little more honest too? "I'm adopted."

"Oh."

He put Sam back in the play yard and lifted Cindy out. "Hey, sweetie."

She nuzzled against his face and he laughed. "I missed you too. But Daddy's going out tonight." Dinner with Max and Kate and their kids was another part of Max's get-to-know the family plan. And now that he thought about it, the answer to his problems with Tory might actually be solved that way too. If he wanted to trust her, he needed to know more about her. He couldn't out-and-out interrogate her, but if the opportunity to question her came up in conversation, he needed to take it.

He glanced at Tory. "My brother and his wife want me to have dinner with them. I hope you don't mind."

Tory smiled with relief. Mind? He wouldn't be underfoot, looking sexy and being sweet with the two babies she was beginning to believe might be the real loves of her life?

She had to stifle a laugh of pure joy. "Of course I don't mind."

"Usually you get a little break at night when I play with them."

"I had a nice break at your mom's."

"If you wanted dinner now, you could go up to the house now. I won't change until after you're back."

"What time are you meeting your brother and sister-in-law?"

"Doesn't matter. I'll call them now and say I'll be there at eight. You just go get your supper."

She nodded, grabbed her jacket and happily left to have dinner with Cook and the other household staff. She hated being excited that he'd be out that night, but she was. It was so much easier to simply care for the kids on her own.

When she returned, he showered and changed while she fed the babies a snack before bed. He kissed them goodbye, told her not to wait up and was gone.

And she had the whole house to herself.

The whole peaceful, quiet, roomy house to herself.

No worry he'd notice she was attracted to him.

No worry she'd feel those things she knew were wrong.

CHAPTER FIVE

THAT NIGHT WHEN THE BABIES cried, Tory raced into the nursery hoping to get to them before they woke Chance, but no such luck. He ambled into the room at the same time she did. Shirtless, sweat pants hanging off his hips, making her mouth water.

She sucked in a breath and headed for the cribs, telling herself to straighten up and deal with this. There was more time when he wasn't home than when he was. She only had to be with him a few hours every day. And they barely talked. When he returned from spending time with his brother, he didn't talk about himself or ask about her. He only asked after the babies. Surely, she could handle that.

He beat her to the cribs and reached for Cindy. Tory almost stopped him, but she remembered that Cindy had special needs at nighttime feeding and showing him would give them something neutral to focus on.

She pulled Sam out of his crib and silently changed his diaper as Chance changed Cindy's. Then she handed Sam over to him and went to the kitchen for bottles.

When she returned, she took Sam from his arm. She walked to her rocker, slid the nipple into Sam's eager mouth and set her chair to rocking.

From her peripheral vision, she watched Chance try to settle Cindy as she fussed. When the baby wouldn't settle, she quietly said, "She likes you to talk to her."

Sleepy-eyed, he glanced over. "What?"

"Chitchat," she whispered, feeling weird sensations in her tummy. His eyes were the color of a perfect sky.

His brow furrowed. "Chitchat?"

"Tell her she's pretty."

He laughed. But when she didn't laugh with him, he frowned. "You're serious."

"Yeah. She likes you. She likes having your attention. So just say nice things to her."

He glanced down at her, pressed his lips together as if thinking that through, then said, "Hey, sweetie."

Tory watched Cindy grin around the nipple in her mouth.

"That made her want to drink even less."

"Keep talking. She'll catch up."

He sighed and frowned, obviously thinking, then said, "Hey. Didn't we have fun playing while Tory went to supper?"

Cindy grinned again.

"I mean, who doesn't like a bunch of colored rings?"

She slowly began to suck.

"And those bears of yours. They're really fuzzy."

Tory couldn't help it. She laughed. His gaze shot to her. "You said to do this."

"And you're doing great. It's just weird to see somebody so…" Sexy. Virile. Masculine. She wanted to say any one or all of those. Instead, she said, "Young. Somebody so young with a baby."

He peered at her. "I'm not that young."

No. He wasn't. He'd piqued her curiosity when he'd said he was adopted, and she'd asked Cook about him. Cook had told her a few things that were surprises. Like his age. She'd thought him to be twenty-eight or thirty. He was thirty-four. She'd thought him to be a somewhat spoiled rich guy. He'd gone off on his own at eighteen and worked in construction before he started his own company. He'd told her bits and pieces of all that, but hearing it from Cook in a coherent order, it had all fit together.

"I'm thirty-four."

"I know. Cook has been here thirty years and she said you were four when she started working for your mom."

He glanced over again. "Really? She remembers?"

"She said you were a cute kid."

He laughed and checked Cindy's bottle. "I could be a holy terror." He glanced over again. His eyes narrowed as if he were considering something, then he said, "How about you?"

How about her? He wanted to know about her? Good grief, they were back to talking? She couldn't remember the last time someone asked about her and not Jason, or the accident, or her leg. And she didn't want to talk about any of those.

She told her heart to settle down. Told herself he

was simply making conversation. It was no more serious than when he told Cindy he liked her bear. "Well, I wasn't a holy terror."

"I bet you were one of those good girls who never bothered anybody."

"I certainly didn't bother the cook since we didn't have one."

He chuckled. She glanced down at Sam's bottle, saw it was half empty and burped him before she let him have the bottle again. Following her lead, Chance burped Cindy and gave her the bottle and the room grew quiet again.

Chance said, "So what did you do?"

"What did I do about what?"

He shrugged. "I don't know. As a kid. Did you like history? Did you have a part in the school play? Did you chase boys?"

Her heart flip-flopped again. His attention made her all tingly. Which took them back to the bad place. The place she wasn't supposed to let them get into. "You should be talking to Cindy."

He glanced down at the baby then laughed. "She's spellbound. She wants to hear about you too."

With her heart beating frantically, she said, “Honestly. There’s nothing to tell.”

He peeked over. “Nothing? You had a totally uneventful childhood, teen years, early adulthood?”

Her face reddened. She wished with all her heart she had a story to tell him, but she didn’t. She dated Jason through high school, went with him to the prom, was injured with him on the motorcycle—

Then spent the next five years either in hospitals or visiting Jason. Not finishing college. Losing her friends. It was like she’d spent those years tumbling down a black hole.

And she finally figured out why she didn’t want to talk about this with Chance or his kids. She wanted a little space in time to forget about it. To be with people who didn’t know. With people who treated her normally, not with pity or a million questions.

He rose from his rocker. “She’s asleep.”

She glanced down and gratefully realized Sam was too. She wouldn’t have to answer Chance’s question.

She hoisted herself out of the rocker. They both

put the babies into a crib. Then he said, "Good night," and she said, "Good night."

But neither turned away.

Staring into his sapphire eyes, a spark of something flickered to life in her chest. Could he be curious about her because he was interested in her? She'd suspected that her first day here, when they stared at each other after he'd assembled the swings and she'd put the twins in. She'd seen a certain glow in his eyes that she'd never seen in another man's eyes.

But that was wrong.

So she turned.

And he turned.

They opened their respective bedroom doors and went their separate ways.

The next day, Chance came out into the kitchen dressed in a suit again. "Good morning."

Tory smiled at him before she slid a spoonful of cereal into Sam's mouth. After a ten-minute talking-to when she went to bed, she'd gotten herself back under control. He'd only been making conversation. He wasn't really interested in her.

She'd made way too much of a few innocent

looks and questions because she was lonely. It was hard talking to someone who didn't talk back. Harder still to talk to parents who wanted her to move on. She didn't need to fall victim to an attraction. She just needed some friends.

He walked directly to the coffeepot. After he poured himself a cup of coffee, he turned from the pot and leaned against the counter. "You and I need to talk again."

Her breath stuttered. She hoped with all her heart he wasn't about to bring up the question she hadn't answered the night before.

She peered at him, her face red. "About?"

"Day after tomorrow's Saturday."

"Oh?" Saturday…she was supposed to have Saturday off. "Oh! That's right."

"You said you have somewhere you like to go…."

"I do."

"Is it somewhere close? Is there a time you have to be there?"

"It's not far and I can get there when I get there."

"I'm only asking because I need to make a schedule for myself."

"Schedule?"

"Do I need to get up with the kids? Will you be back at night or take the whole day off? Stay overnight with your parents?"

She hadn't really thought about it. But her only real priority was seeing Jason. She didn't need to stay at her parents' house. She could come back here. "I could get up with the kids—"

"You don't have to—" He sighed as if frustrated. "I'm just trying to get everything straight that's all."

"Can we play it by ear on Saturday morning?"

He set his coffee cup down with a snap. "Sure."

Then he left and Tory collapsed against the kitchen counter. Trying to pretend she didn't have an ugly accident in her past kept getting more and more difficult. Sure, she didn't want his pity, and she wasn't really lying—but she wasn't being honest either. And this was the second time it had caused an awkward conversation. She had to own up to it.

Regret swamped her. Once he knew, he'd pity her. She wouldn't feel normal anymore.

She squeezed her eyes shut. Was that really

why she wasn't telling him? Because she wanted to feel and appear normal to him?

Oh, Lord. What was wrong with her?

At noon, she pushed the twins' double stroller up the thin brown brick lane to Gwen's. When she reached the mansion, she rang the bell. Gwen immediately answered. Dressed in a chic, classic outfit, she looked the part of lady of the house.

She clapped her hands together. "Come in! Come in!" She turned and called down the hall behind her. "Kate, the babies are here!"

A short brunette in jeans and a sweater popped out of a doorway in the back and raced up the hall. She took one look at Cindy, with a big pink bow in her curly yellow hair and Sam, who filled his half of the double stroller, and she clapped her hands together too. "Gwen, you're right. They are the cutest kids in the world." Then she extended her hand to Tory. "I'm Kate. Chance's sister-in-law. Max's wife." She grinned. "Can I hold one?"

Tory took the hand Kate had extended, her mouth sort of hanging open. Kate was gorgeous, but not "cover model" gorgeous. More like girl-next-door perfect. *Perfect.* The kind of woman

Chance should marry too. "You can hold them both if you like."

Gwen laughed. "We get the babies all to ourselves for the next hour—or two if we can persuade Tory to take a long lunch."

Tory shrugged out of her old denim jacket. "Can't today. Once I eat, it's nap time. I've finally got them on a schedule."

"Then run along," Gwen said, nudging her toward the hall that led to the kitchen. "Kate and I want as much time as we can get with these two."

Tory ambled down the long hall and took the two turns that got her to the double swinging doors that opened into the kitchen. Cook, a short gray-haired lady in her seventies who'd been with the Montgomery family for thirty years and JoAnn, the maid, sat at the long table in the back of the room.

Cook waved her over. "Soup's getting cold."

Tory hung her jacket on the back of an available chair. "You didn't have to wait for me."

"I didn't," JoAnn said, rising from her chair. "Mrs. Montgomery's having a party on Saturday. I'm not just busy. I'm supervising a crew from an outside cleaning service." She gave Tory a hug. "Sorry, but I have to run."

After she was gone, Tory picked up her spoon and took a bite of soup. "Yum. I swear, Cook, you should open a restaurant."

Cook batted a hand. "At my age? Besides, the Montgomerys are like family now."

Tory glanced down at her soup. "I can understand that."

Cook laughed. "Oh, can you now?"

"Yeah."

Cook laid her hand on Tory's forearm. "Why do I get the feeling something's wrong?"

She sighed. "Because something is wrong. Off sync." She drew in a breath. "I'm behaving—different—around Chance."

"Different?"

"I never told him about my accident."

Cook frowned. "So? You want a fresh start." She patted Tory's hand. "No one can blame you for wanting to forget that."

"I don't think that's why I'm doing it. I think I'm doing it because I like Chance."

"Like? Or *like*?"

"Actually, *like* might be the wrong word. I think I'm just attracted to him."

"That's still an ouch."

"I thought he was a real grouch at first. But he's not. He's just somebody who had too much stuff happen in his life. And I think he's just now catching up."

Cook glanced meaningfully at Tory's always-covered left leg. "Like you?"

She shrugged. She hadn't realized it until just this moment but her accident and Chance's babies had thrown both of their lives into a tizzy. And she was catching up every bit as he was catching up. No wonder she felt attracted to him. They were kindred spirits.

When she didn't answer, Cook sighed. "Okay. Here's the deal. You wouldn't be the first nanny to fall for the daddy of the kids she watches. It's almost a pitfall of the job."

Tory laughed.

"But he's not the guy for you. He's older than you are." She motioned around the restaurant-size, stainless steel kitchen. "He was raised in a totally different environment. So what you're feeling is probably nothing more than a good old heaping helping of physical attraction to a very good-looking guy."

Tory breathed a sigh of relief. "That's what I keep telling myself."

"Because you're right."

"So what do I do?"

"Find a way to diffuse it. A way to highlight the fact that he's your boss."

Tory shook her head. "I'm not sure I follow."

"You have to do something that constantly points out that your relationship needs to stay professional."

"Caring for his babies isn't enough?"

"Caring for his babies seems to be part of what makes you like him. So you have to give yourself a distraction so that your job seems more like a job than a family. Like set yourself up as his teacher. You said he doesn't know a lot about kids and you've already been showing him things. So put it in your head that that's part of your job and instead of noticing he's good-looking, start using your brain to figure ways you can help him be a better dad."

Tory inclined her head. "That *might* work."

"It *will* work. All you have to do is stop seeing him as a handsome daddy you're helping and start seeing him as an ill-prepared daddy you have to teach to handle his kids. I guarantee you, it will work."

That night Tory sucked in a breath when Chance arrived home and instead of saying, "Hi," she said, "The kids were particularly good today."

He shrugged out of his suit jacket. "Yeah?"

"I think as a reward for them maybe you should feed them dinner."

"Myself?"

"I feed them myself all the time. You can do it."

"Should I get out of this shirt?"

"I would if I were you."

He went to his bedroom and came out in a T-shirt and jeans. A T-shirt and jeans that made him look a lot younger and a lot sexier than a thirtysomething daddy should look.

Remembering Cook's plan, she forced herself to think of herself as his teacher. She set everything up for him to feed the twins, then stood off to the side, behind him, leaning against the stainless steel stove as he fed the babies.

"I've done this before." He glanced back at her.

"I was alone with them for two whole weeks. It's not like I need lessons."

She winced. Leave it to him to figure out what she was doing. "I know, but the kids like your time and attention. With you feeding and me watching they get both of us, but you especially."

As if to confirm that, Cindy giggled.

They spent the rest of the evening with her looking over his shoulder, occasionally offering advice on what he was doing with whichever baby he had, and just as Cook had predicted, she began to feel better. Like a teacher. Still needed by the Montgomerys, but not so close. One step removed from all processes.

She woke with the twins at two and quickly quieted them so they didn't wake Chance. When they cried at six the next morning, both she and Chance sped to the nursery. But she shooed him out, telling him to go shower and dress for work.

Proud of herself, she had an uneventful morning with the kids and strolled them up to Gwen's at noon. Everything went perfectly well until she entered Gwen's den to pick up the twins after her lunch and Gwen reminded her of the party the following evening.

"Your parents will be coming, so I'd like you to come too."

Having the perfect way out, she smiled gratefully and said, "That's very nice of you, but if you want Chance there, I'm the one left to watch the babies."

Sliding Cindy into the stroller, Kate said, "Trisha, my teenage daughter, is watching them."

"Oh."

Gwen patted her hand. "I'm sorry, dear. We took the liberty of asking Trisha before we mentioned this to you. But Chance agreed."

She checked that both babies were secure in the stroller, not sure what to say. She'd actually love to go to a party. She didn't mind they'd found a sitter before consulting her. But she didn't have a damned thing to wear. And even if she did, her leg was misshapen, swollen. She couldn't wear a cocktail dress without embarrassing herself.

But when Kate said, "Great! It'll be such fun for Trisha," she knew she couldn't get out of this.

And the first paycheck she'd lovingly tucked into her blue jean pocket would go for some kind of dressy pantsuit or inconspicuous long dress that would hide her leg.

CHAPTER SIX

ON SATURDAY MORNING, Chance didn't awaken until ten. But when his eyes did pop open, he jumped out of bed and raced into the room where Tory was playing on the floor with his kids.

"Isn't this your day off?"

She glanced over with a smile, but her gaze fell to his bare chest then crawled down his abs to the waistband of his sweatpants.

At first, Chance wanted to curse at his stupidity, but a very foreign, almost absurd idea entered his head. He liked that she was as attracted to him as he was to her. She was a very sweet woman who loved his kids. In his still-half-asleep state, he couldn't remember why her liking him was bad.

She bounced off the floor. "You're right. It is my day off and I need to get going. I wanted you to get a little energy reserve before you handled the kids by yourself all day. So I let you sleep in." She headed for her room. "But now I have to get moving."

Chance watched her race down the hall and disappear behind the door of her room. Okay. So she wasn't quite as happy as he was about the attraction. But he'd seen the hungry look that came to her face when her gaze fell to his chest. Not to be vain, but she'd liked what she'd seen. They'd had too many of those "we're attracted" moments for him to pretend there was nothing between them.

She came out of the bedroom dressed in jeans and a sweater and sunglasses and his heart skipped a beat. The jeans and sweater showcased her ample bosom and cute, round behind. The sunglasses made her look classy, sexy.

"I'm shopping with my mom and dressing at my parents' house for the party. Kate and Trisha will be here around six to give Trisha an hour with you and Kate and the kids so everybody can get to know everybody before Trisha is left alone with them."

She reached the door, turned, smiled and said, "Bye," and raced out.

He stared at the closed door, his heart pounding in his chest, his hormones racing through his blood like cars in the Indy 500.

Max was right. He couldn't spend his life avoiding family because their dad was a jerk. And—if he took Max's advice one step further—he couldn't spend his life avoiding women because of Liliah.

It had been over a year since she had dumped him. Yet, he'd totally stayed away from women for fifteen months. Was it any wonder he found himself falling for the only woman he'd come into close contact with? Tory might be an attractive woman, but being in a relationship with her was wrong. So maybe the answer wasn't to get rid of her, but to find another woman.

Maybe it was time to come back to the land of the living?

When seven o'clock arrived, Chance hesitated at the door of his cottage. That afternoon Max had gotten him to commit to working for Montgomery Development. That was the good part. The bad part was that he'd now have to hire Tory permanently. And that meant he had to mingle with women. Get himself out there into the dating world so he'd stop being so attracted to a woman who might be attracted to him, but didn't want to be.

Still, knowing he was going to a party with the intention of, well, talking to women made him feel awkward about leaving his kids.

"It doesn't seem right to go."

His fourteen-year-old niece laughed. She had long dark hair like her mom's and her dad's lanky frame. She also wore braces that winked when she said, "We're fine. I babysat Clayton so much I practically raised him for my mom."

He laughed. Clay was her three-year-old brother. And seeing how Kate doted on him the night he'd had dinner at their house, he sincerely doubted Trisha had been as much a party to his raising as she thought. But he appreciated that his niece was trying to ease his nervousness so he said, "I'll bet you did."

She shooed him away. "Seriously. Go. I have Gram's number and your cell and even the cell number for your nanny."

He stopped, faced her. "You do?"

"Yeah, Mom got it for me."

Was it just him or was it odd that Tory hadn't given him her cell number?

True, he could call the cottage if he needed to check on the kids, but what if he needed to reach her when she wasn't home?

His feelings of mistrust rose up in him again and he sucked in a breath. He couldn't go through life suspicious of everyone. If this wasn't proof that he needed to get himself out into the world again, build up his trust muscles, he didn't know what was.

That thought took him up the brown brick lane to the mansion. He entered through a side door and ambled up three halls and a corridor before he made it to the grand foyer. Replete with a huge chandelier, marble floors and paintings worth millions, it instantly told guests his mom had more money than a third-world country.

She spotted him immediately. Wearing a sleek gray dress with a shimmery jacket that sparkled when she walked, she glided over to him. "Darling, you look wonderful."

He pulled on the collar of his tux. "What? This old thing?"

She laughed. "Half the guests are here." She turned him toward the living room door.

"This party's to reintroduce you to Pine Ward. So mingle."

He entered the huge room. Decorated in super modern black-and-white furniture, with white rugs over hardwood floors and a black accent wall, the space was such a departure from the old-style foyer that guests frequently paused at the door.

Chance didn't, he dove right into the fray. If he was getting back into the world of people, he was doing it with gusto. He chatted with his brother and sister-in-law, greeted a few old friends he hadn't seen since he left town and met two very interesting women. Tina, a pretty brunette with huge blue eyes. And Marcie, a blond real estate agent who was so obviously interested in getting his business he didn't doubt for one second that she'd go to any lengths to get it.

But every time he found himself alone, he glanced out into the foyer, looking for Tory.

"She and her mom were shopping today. I'm guessing they ran late. She'll be here."

He turned and faced his sister-in-law. "I'm not looking for Tory."

Sleek and sophisticated in her short black cocktail dress, Kate winked at him. "Sure you are. She's gorgeous and you're a normal guy."

He shoved his hands in his trouser pockets. "The normal guy in me just met two really attractive women."

Kate laughed. "I saw. And neither was as pretty as Tory. Or as sweet."

"Oh, so you think I should get into a romantic relationship with an employee?"

"I think you should be following your heart."

Before he could argue, Tory and her parents entered the living room.

Unlike Kate's short cocktail dress, Tory's sparkly tan sleeveless top with flowing pants showed no leg. Disappointment surged through him. But she still looked exquisite. Breathtaking. No wonder the other women didn't measure up.

"If you go over right now, you're going to look overeager."

"I'm not going over. But if I do it will be as a friend. She's my nanny. I'm not interested."

"Right. You're standing there like you're in a trance or something. Staring at her like a ninny. Because you're *not* attracted to her." She turned him away. "Go back to greeting guests. Make your move when she gravitates over to you but until then try to look like a guy who's enjoying his mom's party."

"I'm not pursuing her."

"Okay. Whatever."

"Kate, she's an employee. An employee who lives with me. And I'm a guy who got dumped by an evil ex and can't seem to trust anybody anymore. She deserves better."

"Chance, you hit a speed bump in life. You came home. You're starting over again. Give yourself a break. Go after the woman who really interests you."

Shaking his head, Chance walked away. He maneuvered to a group of three business associates and their wives. From that moment on, he was immersed in conversations about real estate and architecture, water rights and rights-of-way, deeds and agreements, options and speculation. They carried him through the cocktail hour, through dinner and even through half of the dancing in the ballroom that opened out into the gardens. But again, none of the women he met interested him and his gaze kept seeking out Tory. Until he couldn't find her in the crowd anymore.

He was just about certain she and her parents had gotten bored and left when the people sort of parted and there she was.

She could have been the wife or daughter of one of the wealthy guests who were also his mom's friends. She stood tall, regal in her shimmering pantsuit, not one iota out of place though all the other women seemed to be wearing shorter skirts.

If Kate was right, if he was starting over, if he did deserve a second chance, then shouldn't he go after the woman he seemed to want?

Not allowing himself time to think beyond Kate's encouragement, he ambled over. Coming up behind Tory, he said, "Are you trying to make yourself look interesting and alluring by being different?"

She spun to face him. "Different?"

"Your pants. Everybody else is wearing a dress—"

Her face reddened and he could have kicked himself. Maybe she hadn't known what to wear?

Oh, Lord. He was so out of practice that he'd made a fool of himself and embarrassed Tory.

She cleared her throat. Looking incredibly nervous she said, "I was in a motorcycle accident a few years ago. My leg was shattered. It's repaired and certainly usable. But it's—" She caught his gaze and swallowed before she said, "Ugly."

Well, if this wasn't the absolute worst flirting failure he'd ever experienced, he didn't know what was.

"I'm sorry. I…"

She put her hand on his forearm to stop him from going on. "It's okay. I'm done with surgeries and therapies. I'm fine."

Just having her hand on his arm sent wonderful sensations careening through him. She was pretty and smart. And she liked him and he liked her, but he was a blathering idiot around her. This was why he shouldn't have listened to Kate.

He shoved his hands in his trouser pockets, struggling to think of something consoling to say. But he couldn't think of anything to say that didn't sound trite.

Besides, he didn't want to talk about something that depressed her. He liked her. And since he'd already stuck his foot in his mouth, how much worse could he do? They got along fantastically, easily, when the babies were around. They just needed a minute to get comfortable without the twins.

He held out his hand. "Want to dance?"

She glanced around as if she was looking for a way of escape and disappointment squeezed his chest. Surely, he hadn't misread the way she always looked at him?

He hadn't. In his gut he knew he hadn't. He just had to get them comfortable again.

"Please. I shouldn't have made the comment about the dress. But if it's any consolation, I think I embarrassed myself more than I did you. Dance with me so I know I'm forgiven."

She caught his gaze and her lips twitched. "You're really embarrassed?"

If it would get him a dance and get them out of this conversation… "Yes."

She took his hand. "Okay."

He pulled her into his arms and onto the dance floor and her heart stuttered. Good Lord. It had been so long since she'd been held, felt another person's body against hers. Her nerves popped. Chills crawled up her spine. She shivered.

"Cold?"

"No!" Oh, Lord. Please do not let him think she was cold! If he pulled her closer for body heat she might melt into a puddle of neediness. She was a normal person, and it had been far too long since she'd had this kind of contact.

But it was only a dance. She wasn't doing anything wrong and neither was he. He was her boss. He was being friendly. She was reciprocating.

And that's how she wanted to keep it.

She sucked in a breath. "I like your mom's house."

He laughed. "She does too. But I wouldn't want to have her upkeep bill."

She smiled. "She does like things just so."

He spun her around once. "When we were kids—Max and I—there was no room that was off-limits. But more than once I saw a cleaning crew come in one door as we walked out the other."

A laugh bubbled up. "That's silly."

"That's true. Which is why I'm never going to have a house like this. I don't want Cindy and

Sam to feel pressured to be perfect and I certainly don't want to employ an army." He chuckled. "Can you imagine the mess those two are going to make when they get to be about five?"

She could. She could see crayon markings on the walls, spilled juice boxes, mud pies on the patio. "Maybe you'll get lucky and they'll be good."

He snorted a laugh. "Max was the most perfect child in the universe and he snuck a rat into his bedroom."

She jerked back. "A rat!"

"It wasn't like he found it by the river. He bought it at a pet store."

"But they're germy and they have pointy teeth."

Laughing, he waltzed her around again. "And Max loved him."

She shuddered. He pulled her closer. "Are you sure you're not cold?"

"Um. No. Not cold." She pulled her hand off his shoulder and fanned herself. "Is it me or is it hot in here?"

"Dancing probably made you hot."

"Maybe."

He maneuvered them over to the open French

doors. It was an unusually warm October night and several couples had wandered to the patio and formal gardens. "Why don't we go outside?"

She dropped back, away from him. She cleared her throat and softened her voice. "Really, I'm fine. I should find my parents."

"But you haven't had a drink. Or really very much dinner." His face reddened. "Not that I've been watching you. But I couldn't help noticing that you don't seem to be enjoying the party very much."

"It's a great party."

Kate glided over. "Hey, Tory." She glanced at Chance. "Chance. Wow, it's warm in here. Why don't we go out to the patio?"

She slid her arm beneath Tory's and led her outside. Chance followed, not sure if he should curse his sister-in-law or thank her. She walked Tory the whole way to the back by the rose bushes.

"Whew! That's better."

"It is," Tory said, obviously glad to be outside.

He strolled over. "The moon is nice."

Kate said, "Yes. It is." She smiled wistfully. "In fact, it's so nice, I think I'll go find Max."

And with that she was gone.

Seeing the look of alarm that came to Tory's face, Chance almost cursed. "I swear I did not ask her to do that."

Tory laughed shakily. "It's okay. I just need to get going. I'm sure my parents are ready to leave."

And he would be stuck here for another two hours. Mingling with guests while the one person he really wanted to be with disappeared. It didn't seem right. Everything seemed off.

But he could fix it.

He caught her hand. "You can stay as long as you like. I'll walk you back to the cottage."

Her gaze dipped. "That's okay."

She turned to go again and panic filled him. He tugged on her hand a little harder than he'd intended, and she more or less fell against his chest. Then he did the thing that came as naturally as breathing.

He dipped his head and kissed her. His lips met her soft mouth and needs the likes of which he'd never felt before roared through him. There was something about this woman that called to him. Stronger than fate, more complex than desire, it rippled through his bloodstream and urged him to want more, to take more.

And she responded. Though it had seemed he'd startled her at first, when he opened his mouth over hers, she kissed him back. And he knew, he absolutely knew, she was feeling everything he was.

But just as quickly as she'd kissed him, she jerked away. With two steps back, she pressed her hand to her chest and gaped at him. Her breath panted in and out of her lungs as if she were about to hyperventilate, then she turned and raced into his mother's ballroom.

He ran after her, but an oil tycoon friend of his mother's stopped him and tried to ask him about investment possibilities for the company. Watching Tory slip over to her parents and gesture to the door, he made his excuses. "I'm sorry, but there's somebody I've gotta catch before she leaves."

Chance ran to the foyer but he was too late. A small crowd milled around, saying goodbye to his mom, but Tory and her parents weren't among them.

"Say goodnight to the Stevensons, Chance."

He faced his mother with a smile and did his family duty. He could hear car doors slamming, engines starting and he wondered if he'd have a nanny when he went home.

CHAPTER SEVEN

THE SOUNDS OF TORY with the kids woke Chance the next morning and he breathed a sigh of relief. But instead of jumping out of bed to help her, he pulled the cover over his head.

Had he actually *kissed her* the night before?

Yes. Because he was an idiot. He didn't know what had happened at that party. But he couldn't blame Kate. She'd only read what she'd seen on his face. He did like Tory better than any other woman he'd met. But he shouldn't have kissed her. Not only was he a poor judge of character with resultant trust issues. But also, damn it! He needed Tory. Yes, he liked her. But she was his nanny. He needed to respect their employer/employee relationship and most definitely shouldn't have kissed her!

She'd run out like Cinderella and was probably intending to quit today all because he had no common sense.

He tore off the covers.

Of course he had common sense. The kiss had been a mistake. He would apologize and they would move on.

He rolled out of bed and nearly walked into the nursery shirtless. Until he remembered how his blood heated every time she looked at him, and his muscles tightened. She had a way of making him feel he was the first man she'd ever looked at. If he was trying to stay away from her, was it really wise to see her without wearing a shirt?

With a groan, he grabbed a T-shirt, jerked it on, and headed for the nursery. He opened the door and stepped inside just as she looked up from the changing table.

Their gazes caught.

She swallowed and turned away.

Embarrassment flooded him. He didn't know why he was tongue-tied around her. He didn't know why feelings kept rolling through him, making him want more from her than their boss/nanny relationship. But whatever was happening, it was wrong. It had to be. Otherwise, he'd be smoother, suave, his normal, flirtatious, sweep-women-off-their-feet self. Since he wasn't, no matter what his instincts kept insisting, these feelings had to be wrong. And he would not give in to them again.

He strolled inside as if everything was fine. That he hadn't kissed her. That he hadn't potentially ruined their working relationship.

"Hey."

Her voice was soft, breathless and an avalanche of desire tumbled through him, tightening his muscles, heating his blood, but he ignored it.

"Before we say anything I want to apologize for kissing you. I'm sorry." He moved their conversation past his awkward apology by pointing at Sam who bounced in the walker. "Looks like you're almost done with them."

"Yes. They've been bathed and fed." Lifting Cindy from the changing table, she sucked in a breath. "Chance, we still need to talk."

She wasn't going to let him off the hook with his breezy apology. She was going to quit. And he'd deserve it.

"Please don't quit. I'm an idiot and I swear I won't kiss you again."

She silently passed Cindy to him, and her hand immediately went to the collar of her simple

T-shirt. Her fingers closed around a thin gold chain. When she pulled it from beneath her shirt, a diamond ring came with it.

He frowned.

She caught his gaze. "I'm engaged."

It took a few seconds for that to sink in, but when it did, his heart stopped. "You're engaged?"

"Yes."

He fell to one of the rockers. So much for his instincts that kept telling him Tory was attracted to him. It was no wonder she ran when he kissed her. "I am so sorry."

She cleared her throat. "It's okay. I don't actually wear the ring, so you had no way of knowing."

The dual devils of his mistrust of people in general and women in particular sat on his shoulders and nudged him to forget his embarrassment and go directly to righteous indignation. She was engaged? But she'd danced with him, flirted with him. Instead of him owing her an apology, his demons insisted that she owed one to him. And by God, after the torment of hellish guilt he'd suffered since that kiss, he was getting one.

"It's mighty convenient that you don't wear the ring."

"My fiancé was the driver of the motorcycle I was riding when I was injured."

That stopped his angry mental tirade. Nothing he said or did with this woman ever turned out the way he thought it should. Everything surprised him. It was no wonder he always said and did the wrong things.

So this time he said nothing.

"He was supposed to give me the ring the night of the accident, but…well, we had the accident. He didn't fare as well as I did." She paced away and straightened the covers in Sam's crib, as if she needed something to do while she spoke. "He…um…well, he was really badly hurt. He lapsed into a coma and never came out. His parents found the ring and the proposal he'd written. It was on a piece of paper that was so worn—" Her voice caught. "That we knew he'd practiced it a million times. He might not have ever gotten to say it, but we knew he meant every word. So I keep the ring—" she dropped the chain back down her T-shirt "—here."

He couldn't think of anything to say. Every

time he thought he had a handle on her life, she revealed something worse. Not only did she have a fiancé, but while she was trying to have a night out, probably desperately in need of a little fun, her boss had made a move on her.

"That's where you want to go on Saturdays and Sundays? To visit him?"

"Yes."

"I'm so sorry."

"I am too, you know?" She lifted Sam from the walker and finally faced him. "It's been hard. It feels like I've been on my own for years. And I'm attracted to you, so you sort of overwhelmed me last night. But I'm committed to Jason. I love this job. I love your kids. I was hurt in the accident when I was twenty, so this is the first time in my adult life that I've felt like I was doing something with my life. But I can't stay on as your nanny if you're interested in me."

"I'm not." Yesterday that would have been a lie. Today, it was solidly the truth. He liked her too much, respected her even more now that he was hearing her whole story, to hurt her. "And I love you as my children's nanny." He patted his chest. "I've never been happier."

"So we're cool?"

"Yeah. We're cool."

He played with the kids all morning while she washed a week's worth of rompers, tiny socks and onesies in the washer in the little room in between the kitchen and the garage. At noon, they fed the babies lunch then put them down for a nap.

Eager to continue avoiding each other, Chance made a few calls in his room. When he came out, he expected her to be gone—on her visit to her fiancé. Instead, she sat on the sofa.

Before he could say anything, there was a knock at the door. He answered to find Robert standing on the threshold, a big gray container in his hands.

"For you, sir."

He took the container and Robert pivoted and left. Chance turned to Tory. "What's this?"

"Lunch. I called and asked Cook to send down enough for both of us."

"You didn't have to do that."

"I know, but we had a bit of a bump last night so I figured it was best for both of us to keep talking until we're beyond it."

Not agreeing, since talking only seemed to make him like her more or hate himself, he ran his hand along the back of his neck. "Really?"

"Yes. If we just keep talking to each other, pretty soon the weirdness will be forgotten."

He didn't necessarily agree with that either, but since he and his instincts were so off the mark with her, he was willing to try anything. He ambled to the table and set down the container. While she got bowls and utensils, he pulled soup and fresh bread from the box.

After each had a bowl of soup and a few slices of warm bread, she smiled briefly at him. "So what else do you think we should talk out?"

He shrugged. "I don't know. This is your idea." Then a thought hit him and he squeezed his eyes shut. There was one more thing he'd done abysmally wrong the night before.

He caught her gaze. "Actually, I owe you one more apology. I feel bad about teasing you about your pantsuit."

"That's okay. You didn't know about my leg."

"Does it hurt?"

"When it rains."

He laughed, but she said, "I'm serious. Something about the barometric pressure or the dampness can make it throb."

"It's that bad?"

"It used to be bad. Now—" She paused, reached down, pulled up the leg of her blue jeans and extended it so he could see it—scarring and all.

He looked at her leg, then raised his gaze to meet hers. "It almost looks artificial."

She let her pant leg fall again. "I know. It has something to do with skin grafts."

"Did you have a lot of skin grafts?"

"I had a lot of operations. And therapy. Lots and lots of therapy."

"Sounds hard."

"It wasn't hard as much as I feel like I missed five years of my life. Or I was set back five years. I'm twenty-five but in a lot of ways I still feel twenty."

He nodded as things about her fell into place for him. She might have had a boyfriend who was a sort of fiancé but as she'd said, her growth had been stunted while she spent years in and out of the hospital. That more than explained why she looked at him differently.

And why she was the kind of shy that made men feel bold and brave and protective.

She didn't like him. Well, she did. But not for the reasons he'd hoped.

Their conversation should have brought closure to the feelings rumbling inside him. Instead, disappointment joined them.

But he reminded himself that more often than not relationships didn't work out. Especially his. So he should be glad she was wise enough, or in need of a job enough, that she'd wanted to talk through everything happening between them so she could keep her job and he could keep his nanny.

After lunch, she left him with the babies, taking Sunday off as they'd agreed. When she got home, he already had the kids in bed so she said goodnight and went to her room. He went to work on Monday with the sense that everything had gone back to normal between them.

But Monday evening she had Robert bring dinner down for both of them. As he shrugged out of his suit jacket, she set out plates and utensils. The kids sat in highchairs, banging rattles on trays covered with little round O cereal that they alternated between munching on and tossing.

He tried not to think about how much this felt like the scene he'd envisioned with him and Liliah after she'd told him she was pregnant. Though he hated to admit to the memory, he'd painted a picture in his brain of them as a happy family and Tory was stepping right into it.

A warning bell went off in his head. But he dismissed it. He was a grown man with twins who needed a nanny. He'd been too hurt by the twins' mom to fall face-first into a fantasy. Especially not a fantasy with a woman who'd told him there could be nothing between them.

She pulled the top off the container of hot roast beef and gravy, and the scent filled the air, making his stomach growl.

"Nobody cooks like Cook."

Tory eagerly agreed. "I know! I'll probably gain fifty pounds before I leave here."

He laughed. See? Normal conversation. He knew they could handle this. A little chitchat didn't have to equate to either one of them getting too personal.

"Fifty pounds in eighteen years isn't so bad. Some people do a lot worse."

Dropping mashed potatoes onto her plate, she winced. "I don't see myself staying eighteen years."

"You don't?"

In a voice that was soft and filled with regret, she said, "No. At first I thought I might, but the twins won't need a nanny that long. Plus, I think I'd like to finish school."

She handed the bowl to him and he took it. "Really?"

"Yeah, you know? Before the accident I was taking business classes." She peeked over. "But I love your kids so much—I love everybody's kids so much, that…well…now I think I'd like to be a teacher. I'll need to go to school to do that."

So maybe their conversations hadn't been so great after all? If she was dropping hints about leaving and talking about going to school, maybe he was the only one who'd gotten comfortable?

Still, she was his nanny, not his girlfriend, not the twins' mom. She had no responsibility to them. And after everything she'd been through she deserved to have a life, a dream.

"I think you'd be a great teacher."

"I had some wonderful teachers in school. Especially elementary school. You probably won't believe this but I was a shy kid."

He eased back in his chair and grinned. "No kidding."

"I was even more pitifully shy back then. But my first- and second-grade teachers really went out of their way to integrate me into the class." She took a bite of roast beef sodden in gravy, then wiped her napkin across her lips. "That's what I want to be."

"An elementary school teacher?"

"Somebody who sees what kids are going through and helps them."

His chest loosened and warmed. The feelings that awakened in his system were so foreign he couldn't have named them if he tried. She really would be a wonderful teacher. But more than that, she was a great person. "I think that's a fantastic idea."

"So..." she said, dragging out the word as if unsure of how to make her next point and he knew what was coming. She was going to turn in her notice. When the next semester of school started, she'd be done working for him.

"I'm looking into taking night classes."

He glanced up sharply. "Night classes?"

Her eyes sparkled with laughter. "Well, you don't think I'm going to leave you with two babies by yourself, do you?"

His heart stuttered. Not because she was staying but because she'd thought of him, considered the kids, as she made plans for herself.

She really was Liliah's opposite.

The unnamed emotions bubbling through his system expanded and warmed even more. But in a way that scared him. In a few short weeks, he was beginning to have incredibly strong feelings for her.

Because she was nice.

Sweet.

Everything he'd always wanted in a woman.

But he couldn't have her.

Hell, he shouldn't even want her. If he didn't remain wary, he was going to get his heart broken again.

"You don't have to stay."

"I love your kids. And I heard what you said the first day I was here."

His eyebrows rose in question.

"You said the kids had been abandoned by their mom. You wouldn't leave them too because they needed some continuity. I can be part of that continuity."

His throat clogged with emotion. Could she really be that selfless, that sweet?

She placed her hand on top of his and smiled. "I like feeling needed. I think being here with you and the kids, being needed, is the biggest thing that's helping me to move forward." She pulled her hand back. "Until you guys, I had every intention of spending the rest of my life at home, locked away, not quite feeling sorry for myself, but certainly not wanting anyone to see me. You make me feel good about myself."

His breathing froze. *He* made *her* feel good about herself? She was singlehandedly restoring his faith in humanity. She was so far removed from Liliah it was hard to believe they were in the same species, let alone the same gender of that species. And she believed *he* was helping her?

He cleared his throat. "You've done some good things for me too."

Her smile widened, but before she could say anything, Sam began to cry.

She bounced from her seat and was at his highchair in seconds. "What's the matter, sweetie?" He raised his hands for her to pick him up and she did. No hesitation. No thought. She just reached down, undid his highchair security, and pulled him into her arms.

"You want somebody to rock you?"

Sam snuggled into her, but Chance rose. "I'll rock him. You eat."

"No. No." She brushed him off with a quick wave of her hand. "You eat. I think our sweet Sam might just need a minute or two of private time."

With that she left and Chance sat down again. Cindy gurgled at him. "Yeah. She's a keeper all right. But we all might be in big trouble because she's not ready for what my gut keeps telling me I want." He sucked in a breath. "Hell, she's not even available for what we want." And if he didn't get ahold of himself fairly soon, he was going say or do something stupid again and the next time she really would leave.

CHAPTER EIGHT

WHEN THE KITCHEN HAD BEEN cleaned and the kids were in bed, Tory went to her room. Chance put on his jacket, got into his SUV and drove to his mother's.

He didn't knock, just entered the magnificent foyer and headed for her private rooms. There he did knock. She answered immediately.

"Why didn't you tell me she was engaged?"

Gwen motioned him into her sitting room. "Who was engaged?"

He fell to one of the club chairs in front of the silent television. "Tory."

His mother's mouth dropped open slightly as she sat on the chair beside his. "Oh." She frowned. "Does it matter?"

"Only if making a fool of myself with her matters."

She frowned again. "How could you make a fool of yourself?"

"I kissed her."

Her eyes popped. "You kissed an engaged woman?"

He tossed his hands in despair. "I didn't know she was engaged."

"Oh, darling, I'm sorry. I'd sort of forgotten that part of the story." She winced. "I'd heard about how his parents had found the engagement ring." Her eyes pleaded for forgiveness. "You know I don't like to gossip, but her accident with Jason was the worst thing to happen in town for a decade. We all knew every excruciating detail."

"So Kate knew?"

"Well, yes." She thought for a second. "Honestly, Chance, with Jason in a personal care facility, and him not really proposing, I have to admit that I assumed Tory had moved on. If Kate somehow plays into you kissing Tory, I'm guessing she thought as I did that Tory had moved on." Her brow furrowed. "But for you to be so upset about kissing her, that has to mean she hasn't."

"No. She hasn't. She wears the ring on a chain around her neck."

"How romantic." She caught Chance's gaze.

"And loyal." She shook her head. "What a remarkable woman."

"Um. Thanks, Mom. I'm trying to think of ways to stop liking her and you're not helping."

She laughed. "Chance, you're falling for her because she's helping you with your kids. That's all. You're just grateful. You need to get out and mingle more."

"I don't want another relationship. Obviously, I'm no good at them. And I don't want the kids to get involved with someone only to get hurt when it doesn't work out."

"Then it sounds like you're going to have to start doing things like eat out more. As it is, you're practically playing house."

He nodded. That made perfect sense. His feelings for Tory were probably just an extension of their living arrangement. Being together almost twenty-four/seven did feel like playing house.

So all he had to do was avoid her.

But the next morning, instead of her usual flannel pajamas Tory wore a pair that was soft and pretty. He hurried out of the house so he didn't spend so much time gaping at her. But around ten Tory called him, telling him the babies missed him and hearing her voice turned his heart into a jackhammer.

He had supper with his mom that night, and when he returned Tory was already in bed. He breathed a sigh of relief until the next morning when her sleep-tousled hair reminded him of things that were best not thought about around two babies.

By Friday he was just about crazy from the attraction. He told himself the lust racing through him was undoubtedly the result of wanting something he couldn't have—forbidden fruit. And though that worked, he had dinner with his mom.

On Saturday morning, Tory helped him with the kids' wakeup routine. They played with them, fed them jars of smashed up veggies and fruit for lunch and then put them down for a nap. Just when he would have ducked out to save himself from having to spend too much time with her, Robert brought their lunch down from Cook.

As she opened the containers, he set dishes on the table, his gut twisting with a cross between giddiness and trepidation that they'd spend an hour alone. He was supposed to be avoiding spending too much time with her. Yet here he was, about to have lunch.

"So did you enjoy dinner at your mom's last night?"

He stiffened. Though her voice was soft and sweet, her question was the kind of question a friend would ask another friend. And part of him just wanted to answer. To like her. To be her friend. But he knew how that scenario ended. Every time they got close he wanted to be more than friends.

All of this would be so much easier if they didn't have to live together. But they did. That's how she cared for the babies.

Still, did she have to do things like arrange for him to eat lunch with her? If she left at noon on Saturdays and Sundays the way she was supposed to, he wouldn't be fighting these feelings right now.

Reminded of the stiff, but safe, way his mom ran her house, he decided that maybe it was time he took a page out of her book. His mother, though generous with staff, didn't become friends with them.

"My mother's a wonderful hostess."

"Yes. She is." She filled a bowl with soup and handed it to him. "Anybody interesting there?"

"Yes." Lots of people. But if he intended to put some distance between them, then they shouldn't be talking. He knew his feelings were all being dictated by an unholy combination of biology and hormones. He knew it was easy for a guy to fall for the woman who was helping him with his kids. And she was really tempting.

But she didn't seem to understand. Because she was one of those innocently sweet people, she didn't realize that just being around her tempted him.

He sighed. Sometimes the best way to handle a problem was just to handle it. Say the thing that was on his mind, make her understand.

He set down his soup spoon. "Look. I know my mom told you the story of me and the twins' mom."

"A little."

"Well, then let me fill you in on the rest. Liliah was a selfish, ruthless pain in the butt."

She laughed.

He snorted in derision. "You can laugh because she didn't leave you with twins."

"But you're handling it all very well."

He tossed his napkin to the table. "No. I'm not. Not really. I'm handling things because I have you here. Without you I wouldn't even have swings or a play yard."

"I'm sure Gwen would have—"

"Stop!"

Her face froze and he felt like kicking himself but he kept going. "I have a chip on my shoulder a mile wide when it comes to women. You shouldn't even want to be my friend. And I most certainly don't want to get to like you too much because you're committed to somebody else. So stop. Stop talking to me. Stop being nice to me. Stop trying to make us a family and just be a nanny."

The kitchen became so quiet the drop of a penny would have sounded like the crack of a rifle.

Then Sam began to squawk.

"He shouldn't be up from his nap already!" She bounced from her seat, as if grateful for the interruption. "I'll change him and rock him back to sleep but then I have to get going."

He heard the shiver of tears in her voice and

wanted to curse himself, but really this was for the best. "You have plans for the day?"

She turned. "It's Saturday. It's my day to visit Jason."

Not only had he unloaded on her when he could have been so much nicer in the way he redirected their relationship, but also he'd done it on the day she had to visit her fiancé. He'd known she was going but somehow he hadn't put it all together in his head.

Great. Just great. He had such wonderful timing with her.

He lifted himself off his chair. "You go on. You shouldn't have even helped me this morning. You should have showered and gone. This is the kind of stuff I don't want you to do." He tried a smile. "Okay? I want to be fair to you, but I also want you to be fair to yourself."

She quietly said, "Okay," and went to her room. By the time he was done rocking Sam back to sleep, she was gone.

Tory was so hurt, so wounded, she didn't even turn on the radio of the old green car her mom let her use, as she drove to the personal care facility.

She understood what Chance had said. They were growing close. But she thought they were becoming friends. What was wrong with being friends?

Apparently a lot, since he'd basically told her that he wanted nothing to do with her—and it had hurt.

Really hurt.

It felt a lot like a dagger in the heart.

She'd grown accustomed to eating with him. She'd grown accustomed to chitchatting as they dressed and fed the kids. And, she had to admit, she waited for him to come home from work every night.

Like a wife.

She struggled not to groan out loud. She liked him.

She squeezed her eyes shut. Oh, how she liked him.

But he was right. There could be nothing between them. She knew that better than he did. Staying away from each other really was the right thing to do.

So why did it hurt so much?

By the time she got to the personal care facility,

it was almost two o'clock. She wasn't surprised to see Jason's parents in his room. They visited from ten until two every day and were probably about to say goodbye until tomorrow.

"Hey."

Jason's mom, Emily, turned from the window. "Hey." She walked over and gave Tory a kiss on the cheek. "We wondered where you were."

Guilt snaked through her. If Chance hadn't all but booted her out of the house she would have been even later.

Still, they'd had "the talk" and he'd made her see they were getting too close, closer than a boss and nanny should be when one of them was in a committed relationship. He'd done that favor for Jason as much as for her and himself.

So she wouldn't wallow in guilt. She would simply handle things better from here on out. She smiled at Emily. "I have a job. That's why I didn't get here until now."

Emily frowned. "A job?"

"Yes, I'm a nanny for twins."

"Oh."

Not understanding the censure in Emily's tone,

she quietly said, "Well, I don't really have any education. So there aren't many jobs I can do."

Jason's dad, Nate, ambled over. "I think being a nanny for twins would be fun."

Tory smiled gratefully at him. "It's challenging. That's for sure."

Emily pasted on a fake smile. "Well, if that's what you need then I guess that's fine."

"I don't have health insurance, Emily. Or my own car or even money for gas. My parents can't support me forever."

"You're right, dear," Emily said with another brief, fake smile. She grabbed her coat from the back of a chair. "We'll see you next week then since you're now busy on weekdays."

She kissed Tory's cheek, then Jason's dad waved and they left, closing the door behind them.

She sucked in a breath, turned to face Jason.

If it weren't for the tubes in his throat, she would simply think he was sleeping. His eyes were closed and his facial features relaxed. She swallowed, took a seat on the chair beside the bed.

"Your mother obviously doesn't think it's a good idea for me to have a job." She shifted uncomfortably. "The nursing staff probably told her I wasn't by all week. And she had all morning to brood. So when I told her I had a job, it probably made her even madder."

She swallowed. "But I need a job, Jace. My parents can't afford to keep me forever. And look—" She pulled up her pant leg. "It's not pretty but it's healed. I can walk. Even my therapies are over."

She stopped, almost expecting him to say something. When he didn't, she rose from the chair, fussed with the blankets, tucking them around him. She thought of tucking Sam in the same way and smiled. "I care for two adorable twins. Sam and Cindy. Cindy's like a little peanut but Sam is built like a Mack truck."

She walked to the window sill and arranged the flowers in the vase his mother brought every week. "Anyway, their father is very rich." She leaned toward Jason and whispered, "He's Gwen Montgomery's son. I imagine the twins are going to be very spoiled."

She laughed and wound her way around the room, straightening magazines, arranging things on his tray table. As she puttered, she regaled him with stories about the twins and Cook. She told him about Gwen watching the kids every day at lunchtime while she ate, and even Kate popping by some days at noon so she could play with the twins too.

"Imagine having so much money you can plan your day around playing with your grandkids or niece and nephew."

She laughed. But the sound echoed around the room. Normally, she wouldn't have noticed that, but she'd grown accustomed to noise and sound. To having someone to talk to. Someone who answered back.

And she'd blown that too, by being too obvious or too eager for Chance's company.

Well, no more. As he'd said, there was no reason for them to be friends. They were boss and nanny. Nothing more.

When the sun set and the world grew dark, she unceremoniously left the hospital. Usually when she climbed into her car after a visit, she felt better for having seen Jason. Tonight, she only felt lonely, empty.

CHAPTER NINE

THE SATURDAY BEFORE Thanksgiving the sun was bright and the air was warm. Tory came out of her room to find Chance had fed the kids breakfast and Gwen was sitting at the kitchen table.

"Good morning, Tory."

"Good morning, Mrs. Montgomery."

She batted a hand. "Oh, pish on the Mrs. Montgomery stuff. Your mom and I are friends. You may call me Gwen."

She smiled. "Good morning, Gwen."

Gwen rose. "I'm taking these two little angels to the house this morning because I have a photographer coming by."

Chance said nothing. He busied himself with the kids' plates and a cup of coffee as his mother chatted happily.

Tory said, "A photographer sounds nice."

"I want some good pictures of the twins to show off at bridge club. Kate is bringing her two kids over around noon so I can get pictures of them too, and so we can get some group shots of all my grandbabies."

"Oh, that sounds really nice."

"So you have the day off?"

"Yes."

"Do you have plans?"

"I'm going to do the same thing I do every Saturday."

"And that is?"

"She's going to visit her fiancé, Mom, remember? He was hurt in the same accident she was hurt in. She visits him every weekend."

Though she was grateful Chance had answered for her, his explanation was curt, blunt, almost rude, and it rubbed her the wrong way. Since their conversation about keeping their distance, he barely spoke to her. He shouldn't have the right to act as if they were friendly enough that he could speak for her.

Gwen laid her hand on Tory's forearm. "I forgot. I'm so sorry, dear."

"It's okay." She turned toward the short hall that led to the nursery. "Let me pack some diapers for you and some outfits."

"Don't bother with the outfits," Gwen called after her. "I bought a few things."

Chance snorted a laugh. "A few things?"

But Tory kept going. By the time she came out of the nursery with the diaper bag, he was gone.

Which was fine. Their deal was not to speak, not to be friendly. She didn't care where he went or when he went. She had her own life to live.

She helped Gwen get the kids in the strollers, then showered and dressed for the day.

But when she left the house and saw Chance sitting on the ground, by his motorcycle, polishing the chrome as if nothing were wrong, irritation thundered through her again at his attitude.

She marched over. "If you're not going to talk to me, you shouldn't answer for me."

"My mom and I had talked a few days after the party and she knew about your engagement and Jason. I was just helping her to remember."

"Great." There was only one reason he would have talked to his mom about her after that party. "You told your mother you kissed me, didn't you?"

"I asked my mother why she hadn't told me you were engaged. There was nothing more to it."

"Whatever."

Suddenly she realized she was four inches away from his big black beast of a motorcycle. Chrome pipes, black fenders, white leather seats.

In her head, she heard the crunch of Jason's motorcycle hitting the car that had pulled out in front of them, the shattering glass, the hiss of the sparks as the metal bike slid across the pavement.

Her chest filled with dread and she took a step back.

He looked at her, looked at the bike and his eyes narrowed. "The bike bothers you, doesn't it?"

She wanted to say no. Or "none of your business." Or almost anything other than what she had to say. "Yes."

Wiping his hands on a rag, he rose from beside the chrome pipes. "So, go. Go see Jason. It's your day off."

But she stood there staring. And she wasn't quite sure why, except that a bike like this had stolen her life. One ride. One minute. One *second*. And everything had changed.

"Tory?"

Her head snapped up.

"Are you okay?"

Her eyes filled with tears. "I'm just so damned tired of being afraid of everything."

His voice was very soft as he said, "No one can blame you for being afraid of a bike."

She pressed her lips together, then caught his gaze. "I suppose."

"But you don't want to be."

She shook her head.

"I could give you a ride."

She took a step back.

"Come on. If you were hurt in an automobile accident, you wouldn't stop riding in cars."

"This is different."

"A bit, yes. But a fear is a fear. And you said you're tired of being afraid."

He held out his hand. She looked at it and looked up at him.

"This really is the only way to cure that fear."

She slowly took the hand he extended. He pulled her closer to the bike, handed her a helmet and put one on himself. He straddled the fine white leather seat and motioned for her to slide on behind him.

She actually began to shiver. "I can't believe I'm doing this."

He quietly said, "Just climb on."

She did. As her leg slid over the generous backseat, sensations and fears pummeled her. But she remembered the empty feeling she had every time she left Jason. The feeling that she had no life, had no one, *nothing*, except two parents and the adorable babies she cared for while their daddy worked. She hadn't even been able to investigate schools because every time she tried terror would fill her. Just as she'd fought her parents about getting this job, she was now terrified about taking classes, studying, driving back and forth to school at night.

She needed to get beyond all of her fears, to start seeing the future as something more than a hollow void. She needed to see herself as strong, capable. She needed to stop hearing the crunch and screams of an accident that had happened five years ago.

She needed to do this.

She settled in as he started the bike. It roared to life, shimmied beneath her.

He turned and yelled, "Hang on," then the bike shot forward and her hands leaped around his middle to keep her from falling off.

As they flew down the brown brick lane, the sounds of the accident roared in her head. Terror shuddered through her, paralyzing her. But she didn't feel the force of hitting the oncoming car or the pavement. She stayed on the comfy seat, her arms securely anchored around Chance. Cool air flowed around her, the scent of it crisp and clean. Warm sun beat down on her.

Even as she began to enjoy the sensations, she clung more tightly to him, until she no longer heard the sounds of the accident. No longer felt fear. The sheer joy of doing something she'd always loved rolled through her, saturated her, lifted her heart and her spirits.

He drove the bike out of the driveway and a half mile down the quiet street. With her fears gone and the happy sensations filling her, she suddenly realized she was snuggled up against Chance. Her arms were wrapped around his waist, her cheek was pressed against his back. She could smell him, the combination of aftershave and man.

The feelings that rose up in her stole her breath. Not only was he solid and male, so wonderful to touch, but also he knew her. Jason's parents wanted her to spend every free minute with their son, pretending everything was okay. Her parents wanted her to get on with her life and give up hope.

Chance saw her fear, helped her face it. Knew the real way to move on wasn't to forget Jason but to reenter the world.

A wisp of something curled through her. Insubstantial like smoke, she couldn't quite catch it but she swore it was a piece of her old self, the person she used to be, trying to rise up in her, nudging her to like Chance.

But she couldn't. Not just to protect herself, but to protect him.

He stopped the bike in front of the cottage and she slowly slid her hands off his middle.

Regret filled her.

He turned with a smile. "Better?"

She laughed. As much as she hated that there could be nothing between them, she couldn't stifle the joy careening through her. "Amazing."

He climbed off the bike. "Will you be able to look at this without cringing now?"

"I may even be able to pat it a time or two." Reluctantly, she lifted her leg across the seat and got off. As she pulled her helmet from her head, she caught his gaze. "Thanks."

"You're welcome."

His eyes were the serious blue they'd been the day he'd arrived. Torn. Turbulent. The air between them crackled with electricity. He'd felt everything she'd felt in the five-minute ride. Connection. Joy. And probably the nudge that he should like her too.

She stepped back. He stepped back. She handed him the helmet, then she left to see Jason.

When she arrived, his parents sat on the chairs by the window. They exchanged pleasantries with her and suddenly they were gone.

And she was alone again.

She sucked in a breath and made a tour around the room the way she always did. Straightening the chairs by the window. Dusting the table between them.

"So, it's Thanksgiving next week." She didn't feel odd talking to Jason as much as she felt empty when he didn't reply. "I'm going to my mom's. Chance—that's the name of the guy I work for." She paused to smile at Jason. "Anyway, he and the kids will be going to some big blowout dinner his mom hosts every Thanksgiving. Mom and Dad were invited, but I asked them if we could beg off. It's hard working for a guy, living with him and socializing with him."

She swallowed. Realizing how perilously close she was to admitting she had feelings for Chance, she quickly changed the subject and brightened her tone. "Besides, his mom loves time alone with the kids. With me being gone for four whole days, she will be in hog heaven.

"Not that she'd say hog heaven," she quickly corrected. "She's a bit formal." But not too formal. She let her call her Gwen. And Kate was sweet and Max was funny. It was no wonder it was so easy for her to blend in with that family.

She cleared her throat and began telling Jason stories of the adventures of the twins. When the sun set, she grabbed her coat and purse and headed for her car. She wouldn't let herself even think of how visiting Jason now felt like a job and playing with the kids felt like her personal life. She just got in the car and drove back to the cottage.

Thanksgiving morning, she helped Chance with the twins, barely speaking. With four days off, Jason's parents would expect her to visit on Thursday, Friday, Saturday and Sunday. And she would.

She would.

But they would be long, quiet days.

When she let that thought form, guilt overwhelmed her. She was the one who had survived. He'd taken the brunt of their fall, probably deliberately to save her. And she considered spending a few hours a week boring?

How ungrateful could a person get?

When the kids were fed, bathed and dressed, she walked back to her room, as if by rote. She grabbed the bag she'd packed the night before, slid into her old denim jacket and headed for the door.

Chance popped out of the nursery as she walked by. "Hey."

She turned. "Yeah?"

He reached in, grabbed the doorknob and closed the nursery door. "I wanted to talk to you before you go."

Desperate need exploded in her. If he asked her to stay, would she? Even without a whit of personal conversation between them, she loved being with him and the babies. Her parents' house was so quiet. Her life there just a constant reminder that she was alone.

"Do you need something?"

Retrieving an envelope from his shirt pocket, he said, "Because you were hired by my mom, you were on her staff payroll. We straightened that out this week, and I'll be paying you from now on. But I—" He cleared his throat. "Well, I appreciate everything you're doing for me and I thought I'd just give you the money I should have been paying all along." He handed the envelope to her. "So, here."

She glanced at the envelope then at him. "I'm getting paid double?"

"Only for the six weeks you've been here. Think of it like a bonus."

A bonus worth thousands of dollars! Money she could put toward schooling. "I don't know what to say."

He smiled. "Say thanks and go and enjoy your holiday."

"Thanks." She headed for the door again, but stopped, faced him. Their relationship had become a little better after the bike ride, but the air between them was always strained. She felt bad for that. Felt bad for drawing him into her troubles. But she also wasn't so foolish that she didn't realize how much she needed to be here. "I'm really grateful for this job, you know?"

"I know." He glanced at the floor then caught her gaze again. "And I'm really grateful that we worked everything out so you can stay. My kids love you and I can see you love my kids. A man couldn't ask for a better person to help raise his twins."

Tears filled her eyes and she nodded, as longing flooded her. Dressed in a suit and tie, ready to take his adorable children to his mom's for Thanksgiving, he looked like a proud papa. A sexy proud papa. But he was also a good guy. Chance didn't know it, but he was giving her the only opportunity to be a mom that she might ever get. He was the kind of man any woman would long for a chance to love. She couldn't believe a woman had broken his heart enough that he mistrusted, but she yearned to be the woman who could show him real love.

She swallowed, and turned to the door again. Chance wasn't her mission. Jason was.

CHAPTER TEN

NOVEMBER TURNED INTO December. The weather changed. A day of soft snow flurries prepared Western Pennsylvania for a real storm that dumped eight inches of fat white flakes to the ground. The old car Tory's mom had lent her refused to start two Saturdays in a row and Chance tinkered under the hood until the car purred like a kitten.

So on the third Saturday, after she'd returned early from her visit with Jason, when Chance growled about having to shop for gifts for two babies, she put him out of his misery and volunteered to help him.

"Really?"

"Sure. Even if your mother can't watch the kids, Cook adores them. She'd probably be happy to have them for a few hours."

"A few hours! You think it will take us a few *hours*?"

She laughed. "Hey, these are your kids. Once you start shopping you'll see a million things you'll want to get them. We'll need time to sift through your choices."

His face still scrunched in confusion. "Sift through choices? You're sure?"

"Yes. I'm sure." With a laugh, she walked to the house phone and dialed the number for the kitchen. "Are you busy tonight?"

Cook happily said, "Not really."

"Good. Chance needs to buy gifts for the kids. I've volunteered to help. Can you watch the twins?"

"Sure. Gwen's having dinner out. Technically, you're not supposed to be here, so I really don't have to cook today. Which makes me free as a bird."

She put her hand over the phone and faced Chance. "Your mom is having dinner out. Cook's free."

His eyebrows rose. "So we're good?"

She nodded and went back to the phone. "Do you want to come here since all their things are here?"

"Sure. And I promise I won't snoop."

"You better not. I have your present here and I'd hate for you to see it before Christmas."

Cook chuckled.

Tory hung up the phone. "She'll be here in ten minutes."

"Who would have thought so many people would *want* to babysit twins?"

She walked to the closet by the door to get her coat. "I would. Most people love babies. Twins are double the fun."

A few minutes later, Cook knocked on the back door. Chance swung through the kitchen to answer. "Thanks for this."

She batted a hand. "It's my pleasure." She glanced around as she shrugged out of her coat. "Where are the little darlings?"

"In here," Tory called.

Cook clapped her hands together and ambled over to the swings by the sofa. "Well, aren't you just the cutest?"

Tory had dressed them in red and green one-piece pajamas and put red stocking caps on their heads so they looked like elves.

Cook stooped down in front of them. "We are going to have a wonderful time."

Cindy cooed. Sam yelped.

Tory said, "They're a handful. So if you get into trouble you have my cell phone number."

"I raised six kids. I can handle two babies."

Chance grabbed a piece of paper and began scribbling on it. "And here's my cell phone. Seriously. If they're any trouble at all—"

Cook frowned at them. "Now, you're just making me feel old."

Tory laughed.

"You're almost causing me to consider not reminding you that there'll be no supper tonight since the missus is out."

Chance said, "That's okay. We can easily pick something up." He caught her gaze. "I really appreciate this."

Cook blushed and waved her hand. "Get out of here."

When they stepped outside, the snow was falling as heavily as rain. Big, wet flakes plopped on their heads, their jackets, as they ran to Chance's SUV. They drove to the mall and went to the first store by the entryway.

"Okay, the prices on these are pretty good,"

Tory said, lifting matching sleepers. "But we might want to check—"

He stopped her by putting a finger over her lips. "It's already five. I know the stores are open until nine, but seriously I have enough money that we don't have to bargain shop."

The feeling of just one finger on her lips stopped her cold. She couldn't have spoken even if he wasn't preventing her. The combination of staring into his pretty blue eyes and having him touch her sent desire rolling through her bloodstream on a wave of delight. Not just because of the contact, but because of the casual intimacy. Even trying not to, they were growing close.

"So no bargain shopping…right?"

She nodded.

He pulled his hand away. "And I don't want to buy them all clothes. They're babies. They shouldn't even get clothes. My mom and Kate will probably handle that anyway." He glanced around. "If I'm going to be Santa, I want to bring toys."

She stepped back, smiling. "You're an idiot."

"No. I'm a guy. We don't buy dresses and pajamas for Christmas. We buy toys." He turned her and pointed her in the direction of the toy department. "So, let's go."

They ambled into the small space crammed to the rafters with toys and games of every kind. She gazed from left to right in awe of the fact that there were so many things to choose from.

He picked up a toy gun. "Would you look at this? My God. It almost seems real."

Her mouth fell open. "Oh, no. No! You are not getting your eight-month-old son a pretend rifle."

"I was thinking about getting it for Cindy."

She stared at him for a second, then he grinned and she playfully slapped his arm. "Stop that. Don't tease. I have no idea what you want to get for these kids, so I have to be protective."

His smile faded. "I know. And I like that."

Her heart kicked against her ribs. So many times, in so many ways, they acted more like parents than a boss and nanny. She should have remembered that when she decided to help him shop, but she owed him. He'd taken her on the bike, given her a bonus, fixed her car.

Their gazes caught and he smiled again.

Intense need gripped her heart, captured her soul. What she wouldn't give to be able to love him.

She glanced around frantically, looking for something to break the spell. "So how about new bears?"

"What's wrong with the old bears?"

"See? That's why you need me around. There's nothing wrong with the old bears. But you're building a whole bear/stuffed animal family. Your kids need big bears and little bears and silly bears and normal bears. And let's not forget colored bears."

"We're going to buy eighteen bears?"

"No, silly! You build your bear family over the years. You get them a new bear every birthday and Christmas. Sometimes on Easter. Sometimes on Valentine's day."

He stared at her. "Seriously?"

"Hey, you should be glad kids like bears. They're an easy, no-brainer present."

He mumbled, "I'm going to have to get a house as big as my mom's just to fit the bears," and headed for the stuffed toys.

Laughing, glad their serious mood had lifted, Tory scooted after him. The temptation was strong to twine her arm with his. To stroll down the aisles of toys arm in arm, laughing. Talking about their kids.

But she squelched it. They weren't her kids. Even though she was raising them. Even though she was mothering them. Even though she'd probably never have any kids of her own. Chance's babies were not hers. She could still love them, but they would never be hers.

And he would never be hers.

Her heart broke a bit, but she shoved that pain aside. Lots of people had worse crosses to bear than hers. In many ways she was lucky to have his kids in her life for as long as she could get them.

They chose four bears, a big one and a small one for each baby, then they moved to dolls.

Chance picked up a box containing the popular fashion model doll, dressed in a ball gown. "What about this one?"

She winced. "When Cindy's about six, yes. Right now, no." She reached for a softer doll. One Cindy could hold, cuddle in her sleep. "This is probably what she would like."

Chance smiled crookedly. "Looks like her."

With blonde curls peeking out of her bonnet

and pretty blue eyes, the baby did look like Cindy. Her heart warmed again. "I guess she does."

He dropped the doll into the big blue store bag they'd picked up once they realized how difficult it would be to carry four bears. "Now what?"

Tory led him down the aisles that had learning games for babies.

He froze in his tracks. "Are you kidding? They're too young to be stuck with some stuffy learning games!"

"Learning games for babies are created to be fun. There's music and sound, pictures and sing-alongs." She picked up two games. "Trust me, they will love these."

They shopped for another hour, choosing puzzles and blocks and plastic trucks and cars for both babies.

"They'll love to roll these on the ground, and watch them go." She laughed. "That is, when they aren't chewing on them."

He stopped suddenly and faced her. "How do you know all this?"

She shrugged. "I babysat the neighbor's kids during summer vacation three summers in a row."

"How many kids?"

"Three. From a toddler the whole way up to a ten-year-old, who was a thirteen-year-old the last year I watched them." She smiled at the memory. "The first year, my mom helped. She was next door, so it was more or less me watching the kids and her watching me."

He chuckled. "Sounds fun."

"It was…well, eye-opening."

"I'll bet."

"I learned the mechanics of caring for kids, feeding, bathing, discipline, that kind of stuff. And also the pitfalls. Sassing. Tantrums." She caught his gaze. "Even had a runaway once."

"Really?"

"Yes. Penny, the thirteen-year-old decided to sneak out with her friends." She winced. "She did not think it was funny when her mom arrived at the park instead of me."

"Ouch."

"Yeah."

Chance paid for their purchases and, carrying three huge bags of toys, they headed for the door.

"You know when they get older you won't be able to only buy them toys, right?"

Booting open the door with a nudge from his foot, he grunted. "I guess."

"You're going to spoil them hopelessly."

"Hey, give me another year or two and I'm sure I'll be more than happy to discipline them." He paused, tweaked her nose. "For now, I have you."

Happiness spiraled through her. The intimacy between them shimmered with promise, but though it couldn't be fulfilled, they seemed to have it under control. Now that they'd spent over an hour together, just having fun, her heart didn't stutter every time he looked at her. He never said anything or did anything that went too far. He only made her feel needed—liked.

Was it so wrong to want to feel needed? To feel liked?

They loaded the gifts into his SUV and as he started the engine, he said, "So where should we get dinner?"

She shrugged. "I don't know. I don't care really. I'm starving."

"I am too." He glanced down at the dashboard clock. "And we've only been gone about an hour and a half." He peeked over at her. "What do you say we just find a place and eat there?"

Her heart took a bit of a tumble, but her tummy growled. She reminded herself that they seemed to be handling this. In fact, spending private time together was going a long way to help her see "them" more normally. Just a boss and a nanny becoming friends. "I am starving."

"And we haven't given Cook very long with the kids."

She nodded and he turned the SUV away from the mall. He passed all the perfectly good chain restaurants and headed down a two-lane road that was all but deserted.

"Where are we going?"

"You'll see."

In another minute, they crested a small hill and there on the left was a brown wood-frame restaurant with a crowded parking lot. Adorned with bright Christmas lights and tinsel that sparkled in the glow of the parking lot lamps, it looked old-world, homey and charming.

He opened his door. "You're going to love this food."

She opened her door. "Right now, I'd love any food."

He waited as she rounded the hood. When she

caught up with him, the desire to slide her arm beneath his, to twine them together and walk along the crunching snow filled her. So she shoved her hands in her pockets and headed for the entry. He scrambled after her, beat her to the door and opened it for her.

The warm feeling invaded her heart again. She and Jason had been kids when they were dating. He didn't open doors. He didn't wait for her. But Chance was an adult. A man who was protective and respectful.

As a friend. Or maybe as a guy who owed her for helping him shop.

Nothing more.

A hostess in black pants and a white shirt ushered them to a booth in the back. The lights were dim and when they sat, it was almost dark in their little area. The hostess lit the round candle on the table and left them with menus and the promise that a waitress would be right over.

With only the light of one candle, the booth suddenly felt small, intimate.

Ignoring that, and the jump of her stomach, she opened her menu. She noticed all the usual fare but a sweet spicy scent lured her. When the waitress came over, she asked what it was.

"Three-cheese ravioli with marinara and sausage. It's today's special."

She handed her menu to the waitress. "I'll have that."

Chance handed his menu to the waitress too. "Same here." As the waitress walked away, he smiled at Tory. "So, thanks for shopping with me."

She shrugged, grateful for the chance to take the conversation and the mood in the direction it needed to go. "It was my pleasure. Really. The only people I have to shop for are my parents. And they're…well…kinda boring."

"Count your lucky stars. My parents were anything but boring and they made us nuts trying to choose gifts for them."

"Really? I can't see Gwen making anybody nuts."

"When we were younger she was a perfectionist. I told you we'd walk out one door and a cleaning team would walk in another."

She laughed. "What about your dad?"

He winced. "You really don't want to know."

"Sure I do." Anything to get the conversation off the intimacy surrounding them. Soft mandolin music. Candles. The privacy of a booth with tall-backed bench seats and very little light.

"No. You don't."

The sternness of his voice accomplished everything her good intentions couldn't do. She totally forgot how romantic their surroundings were. "Sorry. Didn't mean to pry."

"No, I'm sorry. You're not prying." He sighed, stretching his hands across the table as if he would have caught her fingers as part of his apology if he were allowed. "It's just not a pleasant memory."

"He was a bad dad?"

"He was bad dad, a crappy husband and borderline thief in business."

She winced. "You sort of mentioned that when Max offered you the job. You said you wouldn't have worked for your dad but Max had changed the company."

He chuckled, but without a hint of happiness. "I'm making myself sound like the villain for disliking him so much. But trust me, he earned my dislike and my mother's and in the end even Max's."

"Even Max's?"

He sat back in the booth. "Max was the one who discovered that Brandon Montgomery was my real father."

"Your real father?"

"My biological father. He told Gwen that his secretary had gotten pregnant and couldn't keep the baby. So he thought they should adopt me, then she wouldn't have to worry about the couple who got her son. At the time they had only Max, and mom had always wanted another child though Brandon didn't. So she thought adopting me was his way of making that up to her."

Sympathy for Gwen filled her. "But he was the guy who had gotten his secretary pregnant?"

"Yes."

This time, she leaned back. "That's awful."

"That's the tip of the iceberg with my dad, who, God rest his soul, seemed to have a knack for lying to everybody."

"But if he lied, how do you know all this?"

"I overheard my dad and Max arguing about keeping the secret when I was eighteen. That's why I ran away. I thought if Max knew, he should have told me. But he'd only learned through office gossip and was trying to get my dad to confirm it. When he did, he wanted him to do the right thing. He wouldn't. Then he died and Max told our mom the whole truth a few years ago. She took it hard, but it helped her to understand why I left and they started looking for me, asking me to come home. That kind of stuff." He shrugged. "When I had the twins, I couldn't refuse them anymore. I needed help. Gwen and I talked it out and realized we'd always been mother and son—no matter who my biological mom and dad were—because she'd raised me."

"That's amazing." Unable to help herself, she laid her hand on the hand he had resting on the table. "And wonderful."

He snorted a laugh and flipped his hand over so he could wrap it around hers. He squeezed lightly. "It is."

"And it's going to make you a really great dad."

"Yeah, if I survive the toddler years."

She pulled her hand back with great regret. "Oh, trust me, the toddler stage is fun and games compared to the teen years."

He laughed.

She smiled at him and once again urges pummeled her. They were so close emotionally that physical needs sprang up without warning. Not just sexual nudges, but the simple yearning to touch. To hold hands. Brush the wisp of dark hair from his forehead. Squeeze his hand.

The waitress came over, setting their food in front of them. Chance said, "Thanks."

As the waitress scurried away and he examined his food, she studied him. He didn't seem to know what a well-balanced, smart guy he was. Considering everything that had happened in his life, he should have been the grouchy guy she thought he was when they first met. Instead, he was kind, generous, determined to be a good dad.

It was no wonder she wanted to fall in love with him.

They dug into their pasta and he began talking about the twins. "You know, one of my biggest worries about having twins is the problem I had with Max."

"You had a problem with Max?"

"He was the perfect older brother but he was also the golden boy. Even if I hadn't discovered my dad's duplicity, I probably would have gone at some point if only to make my own mark, to not have to compete, to be seen as my own person." He set down his fork and caught her gaze. "I don't want to do that to the twins. I don't want them to feel they're in competition. Or one is better than the other."

"With a girl and a boy, I don't think there'll be as much chance of that as there would have been if we had two boys or two girls on our hands."

He stared at her across the table and finally, quietly said, "Maybe."

She licked her suddenly dry lips. She knew what was happening, why his thought process seemed to have stalled. They were talking about the kids as if they were partners in raising them and it was a natural leap to go from that to partners in other things too. The easy intimacy that existed between them imperceptibly led them to the place they really wanted to be—the place maybe where they belonged.

Interested in and mesmerized by each other.

He took her hand. "Would it be so wrong for us to enjoy each other's company…just for tonight?"

Her heart told her no. It wouldn't be wrong.

"You mean like friends?"

"Close friends."

She swallowed. The feeling of his hand holding hers was beyond description. Callouses scraped her soft palm. His warmth seeped into her skin. But that was purely physical. It was the emotional end of it that caused her yearning. She'd felt alone and empty lately, but she hadn't realized how desperately she wanted that emptiness filled.

And, really? Was it so bad to want to be friends?

"I'd like to be friends."

"For one night," he cautioned, reminding her that he didn't want to be hurt any more than she did.

She smiled. "One night."

The rest of the dinner they chatted about the babies, his job, her dreams of becoming a teacher and the classes she'd finally begun investigating at community college. In the SUV, he reached for her hand across the console and held it until they arrived at the gate to his mother's estate. Then he dropped it. He used the excuse of needing to punch in the security code, but they both knew it was as if there was an imaginary line that they couldn't cross.

They drove down the snow-covered lane in silence.

When they reached the cottage, they silently exited the SUV.

He opened the door. She walked in before him and Cook set down the magazine she was reading.

Chance asked, “How were the kids?”

“Two angels,” she said, rising from the sofa. “Did you get all the gifts you wanted?”

In their quiet need, they’d forgotten about the gifts.

They glanced at each other.

Chance said, “We left them in the car.”

Sliding into her big wool coat, Cook laughed. “Hiding them, huh? Well, they’re still young enough that you don’t yet have to go to such extreme measures. A good solid bag will keep them from them.”

“How about if I drive you up to the house?” Chance asked, dangling his keys.

“That’d be great.”

They left the cottage and Tory sneaked into the nursery to check on the twins. She pulled the blue cover up to Sam’s puffy chin, then the pink blanket up to Cindy's. She thought of their reactions to opening their gifts on Christmas morning and wished with all her heart that she could be there to see it.

But she'd be at her parents' house. Then she'd spend the afternoon with Jason and his parents, pretending to have a festive Christmas around him.

Because that was how it was supposed to be.

By the time Chance returned to the cottage, she was in her bedroom.

CHAPTER ELEVEN

THE NEXT DAY, RIGHT AFTER Chance left for work, Robert arrived at the kitchen door with two boxes of Christmas decorations.

"The missus thought you might like to make the cottage cheery for the kids for Christmas."

Tory looked into the boxes with a gasp. Everything from tinsel to Christmas lights winked back at her. In all the hustle and bustle of her life and confusion about her feelings for Chance, she'd forgotten they needed to decorate.

While she set the box on the sofa, Robert brought in a huge evergreen that he set up in the corner in the back of the living room. When it was settled, he took a peek at the sleeping twins and left.

In the quiet living room, she pulled everything from the box and organized it. While the babies slept, she hung lights and tinsel. The twins woke, and she fed them a snack and sat them in the play yard, while she hung the ornaments. By the time Chance came home, she had the tree decorated and the kids were down for another nap.

"Wow."

She clapped her hands together with glee. "Your mom sent everything over."

"I'm glad she thought of it because, honestly, I hadn't."

Neither had she. But as she'd decorated the tree she'd figured out why. She dreaded Christmas. Still, when she'd seen the evergreen and spent the hours stringing lights and hanging ornaments, her entire mood had changed.

Thanks to the twins, maybe she could look at the holiday as fun again?

"I have some spare tinsel and a few ornaments. I thought we could string the tinsel over the archway that leads to the bedrooms and hang the ornaments on it."

"Sounds good."

"Great. Because I need your help. I'm not tall enough."

While they waited for Cook to send dinner, Chance strung the tinsel along the archway and Tory gathered the remaining ornaments.

Unfortunately, even with the tinsel looped low, she wasn't tall enough to hang it.

Chance got the three-step ladder. "Here."

He positioned it below the tinsel and she climbed up. "Thanks."

From the nursery, Sam let out a yelp and Chance ducked behind the ladder. "I'll get him."

After about a minute, which Tory assumed was used for diaper changing, he emerged holding Sam who rubbed his eyes sleepily.

"How's Cindy?"

"Still out like a light."

Tory winced. "I hope she gets up soon or she won't sleep tonight."

Chance stopped. "Should I wake her?"

"No, let's give Sam a little alone time first. He likes being pampered, don't you, sweetie?"

Dressed in a one-piece red romper, with elves dancing across the front, Sam squealed happily.

Tory pointed at the box of ornaments on the sofa. "Instead of me climbing up and down, can you hand those to me?"

Chance strode to the sofa. "Sure." He reached down and lifted an ornament which he held out to Sam. "I bet you'd like to decorate."

Sam made a noise that had to be agreement.

Tory laughed. "You give them to him. He'll give them to me."

Chance held the bright blue ball out to Sam, who happily grabbed it. When they reached the ladder, he said, "Okay, give it to Tory."

Not cooperating, Sam tried to stick it in his mouth.

She laughed and took it from his hand. "Not in your mouth. To me." She hung it on the tinsel. "See?"

He giggled.

Chance walked back to the sofa for another ornament. This one green. When he and Sam were beside the ladder, he gave it to Sam who again tried to stick it in his mouth.

"Do you think he's hungry?"

"He's always hungry." Tory took the ornament from his hand again. "But if we do this a few times, he'll catch on."

It took five tries. Finally, Sam caught on to the game and began handing the ornaments to Tory after his dad gave them to him.

Unable to help herself, Tory pinched his chubby cheek. "You are such a sweetie."

"And happy," Chance said, kissing his other cheek. "He does love special attention."

"They both do. I always try to give each kid at least five minutes of personal, one-on-one time every hour or so." She pointed over Chance's shoulder. "What if we take that star thing and see if we can center it above the tinsel?"

"Okay, but it's a little big. I'm putting Sam down for this."

He walked Sam to the play yard, set him inside with some blocks, grabbed the star ornament from the big box on the sofa and walked it to Tory.

She turned to put it above the tinsel then faced him again with a wince. "There's nothing to hang it on."

"Give me a second." He went back to the box. "I saw some of those sticky tape things that you put on the wall." He reached in and brought one out, then gave it to her. "Here."

Placing the star on the top of the ladder, she took the hanger from his hand and reached up to paste it to the wall. But even stretching as far as she could stretch, she couldn't reach the spot she wanted. So she took another step up, to get closer, and tried again. The ladder shimmied but she took another step up. This time it down right shook. Before she could catch her balance she fell backward.

Luckily Chance caught her. Their gazes met and they both burst out laughing. But within seconds their laughter faded. His arms were wrapped around her. Her arms had looped around his neck, automatically, instinctively, because she didn't want to fall. But it felt so right to be in his arms and to have her arms around him that she didn't want to pull them back.

His head began to descend. Slowly. From the flash of heat that came to his eyes, she knew he intended to kiss her. By the time she told herself to pull away, his lips had touched hers. Softly. Sweetly.

The brush of his lips was a balm to her hurting, weary soul. The well of emptiness inside her began to fill and instead of jerking back, she answered him. Her lips pressed against his, every bit as softly, every bit as sweetly, as if experimenting. It had been a long time since she'd intentionally kissed a man. Though she expected it to feel odd, it was as natural as breathing.

His lips shifted and he deepened the kiss. When his mouth opened over hers, hers opened beneath his and his tongue slipped between her lips.

Sensation after sensation poured through her. The physical ones she expected. The heat in her blood, the tingles that ran down her spine. Those were simple biology. But the emotional ones—the swell of longing, the sense of rightness—overwhelmed her.

She'd never felt anything like this before. Not just a desire to get but to give. To give herself to him. And let the chips fall where they may.

And that scared her.

Because the chips that would fall didn't just affect her, they'd affect Jason. The twins. Chance. The rest of her life, if one night of pleasure caused her to lose the job that was helping her to regain her sanity.

"Stop!" She yanked away and scrambled out of his arms to the floor. "Stop."

Wonderful heat and need still enveloped her. Sweet yearnings that she wanted so desperately to satisfy. Not just for herself but for Chance. That part hurt her, caused an aching sting of guilt she knew would follow her for days. Inside, her loyalties were shifting. She wanted to be for Chance everything that he wanted her to be. She wanted to care for his kids, but she also wanted to care for him. To love him. To be his confidante. To rub his shoulders when he was tired. To kiss away the cares of the day.

But she couldn't.

Tears welled behind her eyelids. She took another step back.

He said, "I'm sorry."

Guilt pummeled her. She knew better than this. "This time sorry won't cut it."

His eyes filled with misery. "Then I don't know what to say."

She stepped even farther away. "That's because it's not your fault."

"Of course, it is. I kissed you."

"I let you." She cleared her throat. "I wanted you to kiss me. I want so many things." Angry with herself and realizing what they really needed was for her to be totally honest, she rubbed her hands down her face.

"It's really difficult being engaged to someone who can't even speak." She swallowed hard. "But I'm committed to him."

He shook his head. “Tory—”

She stopped him with a wave of her hand, caught his gaze. “I don’t know how he did it, but he protected me from the brunt of the fall when the motorcycle hit the ground and slid across the pavement.” The tears hovering on her eyelid spilled over. “He saved me. It’s because he saved me that I can get out of bed every morning, care for your kids. See the sun.”

“And you feel guilty so you believe the way to pay him back is by not enjoying any of those things?”

“No. I think the way I pay him back is by standing by him.”

He shook his head. “No man protects a woman in an accident so that she can spend the rest of her days sitting by the side of his empty body.”

She gasped.

He caught her hand and forced her to look at him. “I know right now you think that everything I’m about to say I’m saying out of selfishness. But, you know what? I’m saying this because I’m a guy. A normal guy. Which is what I guess Jason was. A normal guy.”

She tried to jerk her hand free. He held her fast.

"You're looking at this like a romantic. But if Jason is half the man you think he is, he wouldn't want you to spend your days off sitting by his bed when he can't see or hear you."

"There's no proof he can't hear me."

"You're missing my point. He didn't save you so you could sacrifice the life he saved. He saved you because he wanted you to go on."

"You can't know that."

"Oh, yes I can. Because I'm a guy and I know that if you and I were on the bike and we were careening toward disaster and I used my body to shield yours, it wouldn't be so that you could waste that life." He caught her gaze. "In fact, I'd be mad if you threw away the life I'd given mine to save."

Her mouth trembled.

"The kind of man who inspired your devotion wouldn't want you to do what you're doing. But there's a bigger reason I'm telling you this." He swiped his hand across the back of his neck. "I'm worried about you. How long can you go on leading half a life?"

That hit her right in the heart. In all the years since the accident everyone in her life had worried about Jason. Even her. A mangled leg had seemed like a small thing—*was*—a small thing compared to a coma. So everyone had focused their energies on Jason. His injuries. His needs.

No one had actually forgotten her. But she'd been expected to simply follow doctor's orders and recover. No fears, no emotional needs, no attention. Just recover.

And she had.

She *had*!

Why did this suddenly matter?

She swallowed hard. "Don't worry about me."

"Somebody has to because you won't. I think you know it's time to move on. And it's killing you, but you'd rather suffer than move on."

She licked her lips and stepped back. All sexual feelings aside, and not counting how happy he made her, the fact that he liked her enough to be honest with her, weakened her knees.

She needed so badly to be honest with someone. To talk about her fears. Her hopes. Her needs.

Still…

How did she leave Jason? How *could* she leave Jason?

How could she put herself and her feelings over

his, when she was supposed to be the woman who loved him?

She couldn't.

Cindy began to cry and Chance turned and walked back to the nursery.

She closed her eyes, imagining Jason alone in that lonely room if she stopped visiting. While she enjoyed the twins, fell in love with Chance, made a fantastic life for herself, he would be alone.

She would never, ever, ever let that happen. Even if she was a hundred and ten and had to be pushed into his room in a wheelchair, she would never leave him alone in that cold, empty room.

She swallowed back a boatload of tears, telling herself that maybe it was time to leave this job. But she looked over at adorable Sam chattering to himself in the play yard and another surge of misery filled her. For as much as she couldn't leave Jason alone, she also couldn't leave that little boy motherless.

Chance brought Cindy out of the nursery and she swallowed again. And what about Chance? Would she leave him alone with two babies?

Chance said, "Here's Miss Cindy Lou."

She laughed shakily, swiped a tissue from the end table and blotted her eyes.

When Chance got close enough, Cindy reached for her and she took her from his arms, allowing herself to silently admit that she needed to be here as much as the babies and Chance needed her here. Cindy and Sam and even Chance filled her with hope and happiness. Something she hadn't felt in five long years, something she might not have felt again, were it not for them.

Still, in the days that followed, she withdrew another bit from Chance. But bundled in her coat on Christmas Eve, she glanced around making sure he wasn't in the great room and slid a gift for him and each twin under the tree. Then she ambled to the nursery to say Merry Christmas and be off for her holiday.

He handed her a Christmas bonus.

She glanced at the envelope in her hand. "You know, you don't have to keep doing this."

He put one finger under her chin to lift her gaze to his. "I like you. I know you want to go to school eventually and this will help."

She stepped back, away from him. The kids bounced eagerly in their cribs as if they understood all the things she'd told them about Santa Claus.

Her breath shivered in her lungs. She'd miss seeing them open their gifts. That hurt so much, she almost couldn't breathe.

She took another step back. "Yes. Thanks." Then she raced from the cottage before she couldn't leave at all.

Christmas morning, Chance was awakened by two screaming babies. He bounced out of bed and raced into the nursery. With her hands on the crib railing, supporting her, Cindy bounced up and down and cried unusually hard, as if she knew Tory was gone. Sam sat in his crib crying.

Well, giving his nanny the week from Christmas to New Year's Day off had been a brilliant idea.

He walked over to Cindy. "I'm coming. I'm coming." He lifted her from the crib. "We're all going to miss Tory, but not having her here getting all bound up in our holiday is for the best." Inspiration struck as he laid her on the changing table. "Hey! As soon as we get you two changed, you get to open presents."

As if understanding, Cindy stopped crying. He

made short order of her diaper and then Sam's, quickly fed them cereal and set them in walkers near the tree.

Sam stared at the tree in wonder, but Cindy's gaze followed him as he raced to find his video camera. When he returned to the tree, he turned it on, and the tree lights…but something felt wrong. Missing.

He sighed. Of course something felt missing. Tory was missing. That's why he'd given her so much time off. He didn't want to get her any more tangled up in his life than she already was. It hurt her. And it confused him.

He blew his breath out on a sigh, considered calling his mom to come down and help or even just to watch, but that made him swallow hard. This video would be Tory's only way to see the twins on Christmas morning and somehow or another he felt having his mom in the frames would take away from the intimacy of that.

He snorted a laugh and shook his head at the stupidity of that. He might have been strong enough to let her go for the holiday, but he wasn't perfect.

"Okay, we're all set," he said, reaching under

the tree to get a gift for each child and set them on their walker trays. He grabbed the camera. "Okay. Go. Rip off the paper."

Cindy played with hers a bit. Sam tried to stick his in his mouth. Chance got two minutes of that footage, then he realized it would take all day to open their presents if they kept this up. So he set the camera on the second step of the three-step ladder, about knee high. It recorded everything about the twins and only got shots of him when he ducked into the frame to give each kid a gift.

Even that process took an hour. He hadn't realized how many gifts he and Tory had chosen for these two. But he also hadn't missed one second of the kids' first Christmas. And now neither would Tory.

Thinking of how happy she'd be to see this video, he glanced down and saw a flicker of light bounce off green foil paper. Paper he didn't remember buying. He reached down, pulled the package out from under the tree and saw it was a gift to him, from Tory.

He swallowed. He hadn't bought her one because he worried she'd think it too personal. That she'd feel guilty getting it. The best he could do was give her a bonus.

He sat. Stared at the pretty green package. His heart filled with trepidation. What could she possibly have bought him that wouldn't be too personal, yet would still be a real gift?

Slowly, almost afraid, he tore the green paper. When it opened far enough he saw it was a book. *Avoiding Sibling Rivalry.*

He laughed. He'd said he worried about the kids competing and she'd listened.

She always listened.

She always did the right thing.

And it was going to kill him when he lost her.

But he would lose her. Before her accident, she'd already completed almost two years of schooling. Once she got herself organized, she'd go back for refreshers on her basic classes then only need about two years or so to finish her degree.

Then she'd be gone. And losing her would hurt worse than losing a hundred Liliahs.

CHAPTER TWELVE

WHEN TORY RETURNED ON January second, she felt good again. Normal. Eager to see the kids, but grounded about her responsibilities to Jason. He'd taken the brunt of the accident for her. She would stand by him.

But as soon as she opened the door to the cottage, she knew something was wrong.

Sliding out of her new black wool peacoat—a Christmas gift from her parents—she said, "What's wrong?"

Chance faced her with a laugh. "What? No hello? Just what's wrong?"

"I can feel it in the air."

"It's no big deal. Sam's nose is runny. That's all."

She rushed over to the highchair where Sammy sat. "Oh?"

"We took him to Doctor Nelson and he said Sam was getting a cold. Again, not a big deal."

She kissed his forehead. "Well, it might not be a big deal to Dr. Nelson, but it's a big deal to us."

Sam raised his hands, asking to be held and she lifted him from the highchair. He snuggled into her neck.

Contentment overtook motherly worry. If something was really wrong with Sam, she would handle it. If he only needed a little pampering while he had the sniffles, she would provide it.

"So what else happened?"

"They liked their presents. I've got a video of Christmas morning we can watch tonight, if you want."

"I'd love to." She bounced Sam then smiled at Chance, so damned glad to be home she could burst, but also glad she had her priorities in order again. "What else?"

"My mom showed them off to most of the population of the free world."

She laughed.

"And speaking of my mom, she's gone to Houston to visit friends for the entire month of January."

Tory gaped at him. "The entire month?"

"She hates winter."

"Well, don't we all?"

He sniffed a laugh and walked to the closet for a topcoat to put over his suit jacket. "Anyway, she'll be gone, but Cook's your backup for lunch or if you need help, any help at all, since she doesn't have any cooking to do."

"Sounds great."

Chance turned and forced himself to smile. She looked rested, but she also looked happy to be home. That was enough. It had to be enough. Her happiness to see the twins was all he was allowed. "Good. I'll see you around six or so."

He left the house and made his way through the bitter winter wind to his SUV. He jumped inside, hit the button for a CD and pretended everything was fine. He hadn't missed the hell out of her for the week she was gone. He hadn't wanted to kiss her hello, brag about how good the kids were at his mother's Christmas and New Year's Eve parties. He hadn't wanted to tell her how much the kids loved the Christmas gifts she had chosen.

He wouldn't let himself think of wanting those things because they were irrelevant. But that didn't stop the ache in his chest for something he couldn't have. His only choice was to wish she'd walk away from a commitment that actually made her the strong, loyal woman that had drawn him. And the thought of wishing that turned his stomach.

But he was so alone and so tempted that something had to give.

In fact, he genuinely believed his head was telling him he should continue to remind Tory that a real man wouldn't expect a woman to wait for him under these circumstances.

But his heart simply wouldn't let him. He'd seen the hurt look on her face when he'd suggested it before. He couldn't bear to see that look again.

When he reached his office, his brother Max was waiting for him, sitting behind his desk, as if he belonged there.

"So, here he is, man of the hour with the two cutest kids in the world."

Chance slid his briefcase to his desk and shrugged out of his topcoat. "Your kids aren't so bad themselves."

Max rose. "Trisha's a handful."

"Trisha is *you* about thirty years ago. Just wait till she goes to the pet store and buys a rat." He hung his coat in the closet then faced Max. "So what's up? Why are you sitting at my desk?"

"I wanted to get you before anybody else did. Our partners from Japan surprised us with a meeting this morning."

"Meeting or inspection?"

"They're calling it a meeting but we all know it's an inspection. I don't care what's on your agenda, cancel it. You and I will be playing tour guides all day."

He groaned. "Really?"

"And turn off your cell. Nothing that happens today will be more important than these guys."

He clicked the button to turn off his phone. "Got it."

Max laughed. "And smile. You have two adorable children. You're a partner in Montgomery Development and yet you still have time for your own company in Tennessee. Your mom loves you and you're my brother. These guys think you have it better than Prince Harry."

He snorted a laugh. When Max put it that way, he did feel ashamed for being so down today. He tossed his phone to his desk. Max was right. He had a lot more than most people. He should be happy and shouldn't be pining over a woman he couldn't have.

He walked out with Max, but in the last second, his nerves got the better of him. He couldn't miss the chance to hear her voice, especially if she called to tell him something adorable one of the kids had done. "I'm getting my cell."

Max sighed. "At least turn off the ringer."

After the babies' naps, Tory noticed a big change in Sam and called Cook. "He's listless."

"He has a cold."

"This is more than a cold. I can feel it in my bones. I want to call Dr. Nelson. But I'd also like for you to come down in case Doc wants me to bring him into the office for another checkup."

"I'll be there in ten minutes."

She called Dr. Nelson's office, and as she suspected they wanted her to bring Sam in. As Cook slid him into a snowsuit, she put on her peacoat, grabbed her cell and speed dialed Chance's number. In four rings, it went to voice mail.

"I don't want to scare you, but Sam didn't look very well after his nap so I called Dr. Nelson and he wants to see him again this morning."

She paused, giving herself a second to get the panic out of her voice. She seriously hoped there was nothing wrong with her sweet baby boy, that his listlessness was only another symptom of his cold, but she had a horrible, horrible feeling that it was more and she couldn't shake it. "So call me when you get this."

Cook put Sam in her arms and she raced out to her car, but Robert was already in the driveway with Gwen's SUV. He opened the back door, revealing her twin car seats.

"The Missus likes to be prepared and I don't want you driving."

She smiled her thanks. "I appreciate this." Then she slid Sam into his car seat and ran to the passenger's side door.

Robert had them in town in only a few minutes. He parked in front of the building housing the doctor's office and helped her get Sam out of his seat because her hands were shaking.

At the window for the receptionist, she said, "I called Dr. Nelson this morning. Sam is sick." Her eyes filled with tears. "He said to bring him right in."

A nurse appeared at the door to the right and

motioned for Tory to come back to an exam room. Once inside, the nurse took Sam and unzipped his snowsuit. "Hey, sweet Sammy," she crooned, obviously familiar with the baby. "We saw Sam two days ago when Chance brought him in." She smiled. "I'm guessing you're the nanny."

Tory nodded.

"He signed papers for you to authorize treatment."

She breathed a sigh of relief, then pulled her cell phone from her jacket pocket. She hit the speed dial for Chance's cell phone, but again it went to voice mail.

"Sammy," the nurse crooned again, trying to wake him, just as Dr. Nelson entered the room.

"Now, what this I hear about Sam being sick again?"

The nurse gave the doctor a meaningful glance as she laid the baby on an exam table that looked like one of their changing tables at home. The doctor walked over and opened both of Sam's eyes, peering into them, then he whispered something to the nurse who raced out of the room.

"You're Tory, right?"

Tory nodded.

"Okay. I need you to call Chance. I'm sending Sam to the hospital."

When Chance put on his jacket after a two-hour lunch, he felt his cell phone vibrating. Unfortunately, the call went to voice mail before he could answer it. That was when he noticed he had eight missed calls.

He heard the shiver of fear in Tory's voice when he listened to the first message saying they were going back to Dr. Nelson's office. And she was crying by the time he got to message number eight, the one when she told him Sam was at the hospital and she was in a waiting room and she hadn't heard anything from anybody for forty minutes.

He didn't even say goodbye to Max or their guests. He ran to his office, got his topcoat and keys and left for the hospital. He called Tory and she tearfully told him she was in the third floor waiting room with Robert and he should meet her there.

It seemed to take forever for the elevator to get him to the third floor. As he stepped out, he saw

Tory, pacing in the hall. She turned and saw him and the next thing he knew she was in his arms sobbing.

"I don't know what happened! I don't know what's wrong!"

She clung to him, obviously sharing the same desperation that raced through his blood. He slid his lips over her hair, her forehead. "It's fine. Everything will be fine." Though deep down inside he didn't know anything of the sort. All he knew was his baby was sick, they were both scared to death and in his heart he knew he had to comfort her.

"Let's not panic until we hear from the doctor."

She began to shiver. "But it's never good news. Never good news!"

Though fear for Sam still paralyzed him, he suddenly realized Tory's fears were a hundred times worse. She'd been here. Probably this very hospital. With a shattered leg and a dying boyfriend.

He smoothed his hand down her hair. "Hey. Shh. It's going to be okay. Dr. Nelson is the best."

Even as he said that, Dr. Nelson walked out of a swinging door. "Chance. I see you made it."

The very fact that his voice was calm sent a river of relief through Chance. Still, when he turned to face the doctor, he kept his arm around Tory, supporting her. "Stupid meetings. My brother told me to turn off my cell—" He sucked in a breath. "How is he?"

"He's fine. His fever got to him. Apparently the meds we prescribed didn't take his fever down enough. We have it down now, but I'd like him to spend the night." He smiled. "Just in case."

Chance wanted to collapse with relief. Tory gasped twice then threw herself into his arms again and wept. Dr. Nelson said, "He's in room 312 when you're ready." Then he turned and walked over to the nurse's station.

Chance squeezed Tory against him. He felt everything she felt, wanted to cry as much as she did, and simply basked in the fact that he wasn't alone. Neither was she. They had each other.

They had each other.

But they didn't really.

She belonged to someone else and every time he held her or kissed her, he trespassed.

He eased back, setting her a few feet away from him.

She smiled sheepishly at him. “I’m so sorry.”

“For?”

“I panicked. I got emotional.”

He smiled ruefully. He didn’t want to remind her that this hospital probably brought back terrible memories for her. Instead, he directed the conversation as far away from Jason and her accident as he could. “I like that you’re emotional about my kids. It means you love them. It means they get the benefit of that every day.”

She shook her head, and smiled, then caught his gaze again. But after only a second, her smile faded. Her eyes filled with wonder, she put her hand on his cheek, feathered her fingers along his jawline.

It was as if she was seeing him for the first time. Or maybe realizing for the first time how close they’d become.

He held perfectly still. Didn’t even breathe. He wanted this woman so much that it hurt to even think about it. And he wouldn’t jeopardize what was happening right now by saying or doing something that would break the trance she seemed to be in.

She stretched forward and placed her lips on

his. Softly. Easily. Then she pulled back, studying his eyes again.

He tried to tell her everything he felt without saying a word. That he needed her. That he loved how good she was with his kids. That there was something between them that should be explored.

But she took another step away from him and he knew that even if he'd gotten through it didn't matter. She had commitments she wouldn't break.

It nagged at him. As she slept on a chair in Sam's room that night, Chance stood by the window, staring out. Snow twinkled in the streetlights that illuminated the cars in the parking lot.

He couldn't figure out if Tory was being torn apart or managing to straddle two worlds. One world, her life with Jason, was sad. Probably empty. The world she shared with him was filled with laughter and noise.

He supposed they probably balanced out—for her.

For him, there was a perpetual *what if.* A promise of something wonderful that teased him, even as it reminded him there could never be anything more.

He walked to his chair, sat down and rubbed his

hands down his face. The really sad part about this was he knew Tory's loyalty to her fiancé was part of what drew him. Take away that loyalty and would she be the same woman?

Yes.

Because the time had long passed since her debt, her commitment, to her fiancé had been paid. And in his heart he knew that no man would want a woman to stand by his impotent body year after year to keep a commitment that could no longer be honored.

And the more he got to know Tory, the more he felt for her, the more he wondered if Fate hadn't tossed her in his path to tempt her back to her real life.

Not that he thought he was any wonderful temptation when they'd first met. But what they had now was.

How could he tell her so that she'd listen?

They'd already had this conversation once and she'd blown him off.

Should he try again?

Or should he pray that what he'd already said would someday sink in?

* * *

They brought Sam home from the hospital the following day. The second they entered the cottage, Cindy began to squawk. Thinking she was tired of Cook and missing him, Chance raced over and took her from Cook's arms.

But Cindy kept squawking.

Until Tory walked over with sleeping Sam.

Cindy patted his face and cooed and Cook gasped. "Isn't that adorable? She missed him."

"I never thought about it," Chance said, as he held Cindy close enough to pat Sam. "But I don't think they've ever spent a day apart."

"She wasn't fussy last night," Cook said. "Slept like an angel. But this morning she was crazy."

"She missed her brother," Tory agreed. "But right now we need to get him into his crib."

Chance caught her gaze. "Maybe we could put them down for a nap together."

She smiled and nodded. "It would give them a sense of normalcy."

They put sleeping Sam into his crib and Cindy in her crib and that seemed to be enough for Cindy who settled in to sleep.

Chance headed to the door but instead of

following him, Tory took a seat on one of the rockers.

"Aren't you coming?"

"I just want to sit here for a while."

Chance sighed. "I know you're tired. If nothing else your muscles are probably cramped from sleeping in that chair. Why don't you just—"

She settled on the rocker. "I'm fine."

"Tory, we've got the baby monitor on. And our bedrooms are two feet away. You get a shower first. I'll take one second—"

She shook her head. "I want to stay here."

He closed his eyes, then headed out.

He didn't have to have the conversation with her about her loyalty. If she wouldn't leave a sleeping baby who'd gotten a clean bill of health, she'd never even consider leaving Jason.

CHAPTER THIRTEEN

VALENTINE'S DAY ARRIVED with Artic temperatures and a burst of snow. Chance reluctantly rolled out from under his warm covers to the sound of icy precipitation pelleting his bedroom window.

One of the twins squawked and he paused, listening more closely. But he didn't hear anything except Sam's squeals and Cindy's soft crying.

Tory must not be up yet.

He rubbed his hands together with glee. That was perfect. He might not be able to love Tory the way he wanted, but he did love her and there was no way in hell he would let her go through a Valentine's Day without letting her know she was special.

He sneaked into the nursery in stocking feet and put a finger over his lips, silently telling the twins to settle down.

"We don't want to wake Tory."

Cindy cocked her head. Sam frowned.

"Come on. I can change you both without either one of you crying, if nobody gets impatient."

Knowing Cindy was the quieter crier, he changed Sam first, then Cindy, and carried both to the kitchen and put them into the highchairs.

He quickly threw together a pot of coffee and started searching for a frying pan. After retrieving one from the lower cupboard, he set it on the stove, dropped in a lump of butter and headed to the refrigerator for eggs.

Sam squealed.

He pivoted to face him. "Hey, we're making Tory a surprise breakfast in bed. You'll get fed when she gets fed."

Sam's squeal became a squawk.

He laughed. "You will not die if you have to wait five minutes for your food."

As bread toasted, he made enough scrambled eggs for Tory, himself and two babies.

Sam began pounding on his highchair tray.

"Shh! I need five more minutes at most. Surely, you can give me five minutes."

Sam growled. Chance laughed as he went in

search of a bed table and the rose he'd bought the night before and hidden in his room.

With two plates of eggs and toast on the bed table along with a red stuffed bear and a slim vase with the one red rose, he turned to get the babies. His eyes narrowed.

How was he going to carry two kids and a bed table?

Inspiration struck and he got the stroller. He tucked the babies inside. Carrying the tray in one hand, he pushed the stroller with the other.

At her door, he knocked lightly. "Tory?"

He waited a few seconds but heard nothing. So he knocked again. This time he heard, "Oh, my God! I'm sorry. I slept in!"

"Don't worry about it. Are you decent?"

Silence. Then, sounding confused, she said, "I'm in pajamas."

"Great." With a quick push, he opened the door and strolled in the babies.

"We brought you breakfast in bed—" He stopped. She lay on her pillows with her covers tucked under her neck. "I thought you were decent?"

"I am. But I'm confused. Why would you bring me breakfast in bed?"

"Because it's Valentine's Day."

Panic flitted across her face. She tightened her grip on the covers at her chin.

He quickly said, "None of this is from me. It's from the babies."

Sam squeaked. Cindy giggled.

"And they are really hungry and my arm is breaking."

Her face softened. She pushed her covers aside and walked to the stroller. Stooping in front of the kids she said, "You did that for me?"

"Yes. They did this. All by themselves. For you. But if you get out of bed, then it's all wasted."

She turned and scrambled under the covers again. He set the bed table across her lap, then he got the kids.

As he placed Cindy on the bed beside Tory, she picked up the bear. "There's a bear."

He turned away to get Sam. "The kids picked that out too. You said everybody should have a bear family. They decided it was time to start yours."

He plopped Sam on the bed. He headed straight for the tray.

Chance caught him by the pajama bottoms and hauled him back. "Hey, mind your manners."

Tory laughed.

Chance said, "You feed Cindy. I'll feed Sam."

She nodded, picked up a fork and eased a bite of scrambled eggs into the little girl's mouth. "Thank you for the breakfast in bed."

Cindy grinned.

"And the bear."

Sam yelped.

Chance said, "Don't think you're stealing that."

Sam squealed and Chance silenced him with a forkful of scrambled eggs. He smacked his lips greedily.

Feeding Cindy, Tory nibbled on a piece of toast and Chance relaxed. She liked the Valentine's treat from the kids. He hadn't overstepped any boundaries. Yet he'd accomplished what he'd set out to do. No woman who was as loved as she was should be ignored on Valentine's Day.

She patted the bed beside her and caught his gaze. "Sit. You can't feed him standing up like that."

He lifted Sam from the bottom of the bed and took a cautious step toward the top as she lifted the bed table off her lap and scooted across the bed to the other side.

He sat, settled Sam on his lap and then adjusted the pillow behind his back. With the tray between them, he smiled at Tory. “Thanks.”

Her gaze dipped, then she seemed to gather her courage and she looked at him again. “No. Thank you.”

“What? Me? The twins did all this. I just had to reach into the cupboards for the high stuff.”

She laughed.

Cindy patted the bed table, obviously asking for another bite. Chance gave Sam a forkful of eggs before he reached for one of the slices of toast.

“There’s coffee in the kitchen. I didn’t want to risk spilling it on your bed.”

Tory chuckled. “Good idea.”

Chance settled against the headboard. The kids were happy. He was ecstatic. And Tory looked comfortable. Happy. Happier than he’d ever seen her. He’d saved her from a disastrous Valentine’s Day.

The house phone on the night table beside Tory

trilled. Balancing Cindy across her thighs, she hit speaker.

"Cook?"

"Um. No, darling, it's me, Gwen."

"Hey, Gwen! Do you want to talk to Chance? He's right here. I have the phone on speaker."

"No. I just called because I sent visitors down to the cottage."

Chance said, "Visitors? At seven in the morning?"

"It's Jason's parents, darling. They need to talk to Tory."

Tory froze.

Chance said, "Thanks, Mom."

He clicked off the speaker function and wrestled with a long string of curses. Of all the days or times for Jason's parents to decide to check out her job, this was the worst.

He rolled off the bed, taking Sam with him. "I'll carry the kids to the nursery."

She rolled out on the other side. "I'll take the bed table to the kitchen."

Already around to her side of the bed, he grabbed Cindy from her arms. She reached for the tray table and the red bear bumped her hand.

She glanced up at Chance. He looked down at her. They both knew who'd gotten her the bear, who'd made the breakfast. And they both knew why.

She eased the bear off the tray and dropped it to the bed.

Then he raced to the nursery and she raced out to the kitchen.

He heard the knock on the door and, suddenly, he couldn't let her face Jason's parents alone. Yes, everybody was still in his or her respective pajamas. But it was seven o'clock in the morning. People who visited a home with twin babies at seven o'clock in the morning got what they got.

Angry, defensive, he strode into *his* living room with *his* twins to protect *his*…nanny.

The door opened and on the threshold stood an older man and woman. The woman held a crumpled tissue. It was clear both had been crying.

"Nate? Emily?" When neither said a word, Tory eased back, opening the door a little wider. "Come in."

Nate glanced at Chance and his two pajama-clad babies. He smiled wryly. "We should have called."

Chance took a few steps into the great room, set the babies in the play yard and said, "No. We're fine. We were up." He headed for the kitchen. "Can I get you some coffee?"

Emily said on the sofa. "No. Thank you." She glanced at Tory. "Tory, dear, could you sit, please?"

As if frozen with fear, Tory sat on the recliner. Chance's heart accelerated. Jason's parents were here. Crying.

His chest tightened with misery and guilt. And god-awful hope for which he hated himself. Except, if Jason was the man he thought he was, he wouldn't want to live for thirty years in a coma. If he had passed, death had been welcome for him.

Tory quietly said, "What's wrong?"

"Jason had a stroke last night."

Tory said, "Oh!" She pressed her hand to her mouth. "Oh, my God."

"He's stable," Nate said.

Squeezing his eyes shut, Chance quietly cursed. The last thing that man wanted was to hang on. This time the misery he felt was misery for Jason.

Needing something to do, he filled four cups with coffee, then removed the plates from the bed tray he'd used for Tory's breakfast and set the coffee, cream and sugar on it.

As he walked toward the sofa, Nate said, "I'm sorry, Tory."

Sobbing quietly, Tory said, "Don't feel sorry for me. It's Jason I worry about."

Nate reached across the coffee table and caught Tory's hand. "Honey, the reason Emily and I are here isn't to tell you about the stroke." He swallowed then cleared his throat. "This morning the doctors talked to us about turning off life support."

She gasped. Tears that had been hovering on her eyelids spilled over. "No!" She bounced out of her chair. "No!"

Chance set the coffee on the table between the chairs and the sofa. He drew Tory into his arms. "Hey. Don't say anything. Just cry for a minute."

His own throat closed. He could not imagine what she was going through, but he did know that if somebody had told him they were considering turning off Tory's life support, he probably would have punched them.

Emily and Nate rose. Nate said, "We wanted to tell you in person. Damage from the stroke was extensive. He's at Mercy Hospital where they did the testing. They're saying he's gone, Tory. Really gone this time."

Holding sobbing Tory, Chance pressed his lips together and nodded to them.

Emily began to cry too.

Nate wrapped his big arm around his wife's shoulders. "And no decision has been made yet."

Chance caught Nate's gaze. The look they exchanged was very telling. The decision might not be final, but it had been made.

And it had been made because they had no choice.

Nate and Emily left quietly as Tory clung to him. When she pulled away, the tracks of her tears shimmered on her cheeks. "I better get dressed."

"You can stay in your pajamas as long as you want today. I'll stay home with the kids."

She gazed up at him. "But I have to go to the hospital to see Jason."

Of course she would. How could he not have thought of that? "I'll drive."

"You have the kids."

"Mom or Cook will take the kids."

But after Tory had dressed in jeans and a pretty red sweater, and returned to the great room, she immediately reached for Sam and hugged him. Sam let out with a yelp, as if she'd squeezed him too tightly and she laughed.

Laughed.

On a day when her heart had clearly been shattered, she had laughed because she loved these kids. And they loved her and maybe they were enough to remind her that one part of her life might be ending, but she still had the twins—still had him.

He ambled over. "Mom has a lunch date and Cook has somewhere to be this morning. So I thought we'd take the kids."

She peered over at him. "Really? To a hospital?"

"Hospital rules are a lot less strict than they used to be. And who knows? Maybe seeing them might cheer up Jason, too."

She brightened at that, helped him stuff the babies in their snuggly snowsuits and snap them into their car seats. He followed her into the hospital, as she wove down corridors and switched elevators and finally went into a room so quiet there was no sound but the beeps and swishes of the machinery attached to the man on the bed.

Holding Cindy, Tory walked in first. "Hey, Jason, look who I have! It's one of the twins I've been telling you about." She ambled to the bed. "This is Cindy." She kissed Cindy's cheek. "Say hello, sweetie."

Cindy let out with a sound halfway between a coo and a bark. Tory laughed.

Chance would have laughed too, except he couldn't stop staring at the man on the bed. Tubes were everywhere. IVs and breathing tubes. Little pasty things were attached to his head and chest. His eyelids didn't even flutter.

He had to turn away, but Tory brightly walked around the room. Still holding Cindy, she straightened the few items on the tray table beside the bed and then the bedside table itself.

"It looks like things are very quiet here today." She partially unzipped Cindy's snowsuit. "But it's sort of quiet everywhere. It snowed last night so everyone is driving slower and the people who don't have to go out aren't going out."

She laughed as if he'd answered, and Chance's heart broke.

"I know. I know. If I'd learn to ski I'd love snow too." She laughed again, bounced Cindy on her hip. "But I'd rather be happy in my quiet dislike of winter. Because—" she smiled at him "—that just makes me love summer more.

"And I do love summer." She suddenly glanced over and saw Chance standing in the doorway to the room, holding Sam. "Oh, Jason. I almost forgot to introduce you to Sam." She motioned for him to come in. "And the twins' daddy, my boss, Chance Montgomery."

Chance smiled and said, "Hello," because, as she'd told him before, they didn't really know if Jason could hear or not. And if it helped her get through this situation, then he would simply go along.

A nurse in white scrubs dotted with pink and red Valentine's Day hearts shuffled in, looking at a chart. When she glanced up and saw him, Tory and two babies, she gasped. "You can't be in here."

Tory said, "It's okay. They're with me."

"Jason's only allowed one visitor at a time. Two, when his parents are here."

The nurse faced Chance and Chance gave her a pleading look.

"Okay, one minute for everyone to say goodbye, then everybody but Tory leaves."

He nodded.

The nurse looked at the IV bag, made some notes and scurried away.

Chance moved closer to Tory, extending his arm to take Cindy. "The kids and I will wait in the cafeteria. Stay as long as you want."

She smiled gratefully then her eyes suddenly filled with tears. "Thanks. It was nice of you to bring them along."

He walked to the door but faced her again. Her happy expression was gone. All the sadness in her heart was evident in her eyes as she gazed at Jason.

And Chance knew the kids had made a difference. Maybe they gave her a way to focus on the future? Maybe they gave her a way to focus on something good? Maybe she just liked having them in her arms? Whatever the reason, she needed them.

* * *

He left the room and Tory sat on the chair beside Jason's bed. "This is hard, Jace."

He said nothing. And not only did he say nothing, but the room felt empty, devoid of his presence. Coldness swept through her. Bitter and frightening, it tightened her muscles, squeezed her heart.

So she jumped to the topic that always warmed the room. "Did you like the twins?" She laughed, or tried. Without the sense that he was listening, happiness was elusive, her efforts strained. "They, um, keep me hopping."

She rose and walked to the window. Slatted blinds let only the tiniest amount of sun in, so she opened them.

"Actually, over the past few months, they've kept me from going crazy." She faced the bed again. "You can't imagine how hard this has been. I've been so alone for the past five years… Still, when Mom suggested I get a job, I fought it. Then I met the twins, and it was like I had sunshine in my life for the first time. They're so alive. So vibrant. And so full of promise."

She stopped. *Promise.* Actually, it was Chance who filled her life with promise. He'd listened when she talked about night classes. He'd helped her investigate a few schools. The kids made her laugh, but he made her happy.

Warmth seeped into her frozen soul, melted her heart, made breathing easy again.

While Jason lay on a bed dying.

And it didn't matter what she said or did. It didn't matter if every doctor in this hospital came into this room right now and did their very, very best to save him. He was dying.

Tears flooded her eyes. She walked back to the bed, took his hand as sobs tore through her chest. She let herself cry until there were no more tears, then she leaned in, kissed his cheek.

Stepping away, she let his hand fall to the bed. It did so lifelessly.

Chance suddenly appeared at the door. Chance, the guy who was always there for her.

For her.

There was no one who could help Jason. But she had Chance.

"Sorry to interrupt, but the nurses really need to be in here now."

She glanced over at him. "Where are the twins?"

"They're top billing at the nurse's station."

"Top billing?"

"They're entertaining."

She laughed. He held out his hand. "So, are you ready?"

She smiled slightly and nodded, because her mind had been made up. She walked to him, but didn't take his hand. She led him out of Jason's room, over to the nurse's station where she took Cindy, thanked everyone for their kindnesses to the kids and Jason, and left.

She was silent, a virtual zombie, the entire drive home, but Chance wasn't worried. They'd been at the hospital nearly three hours. They'd whipped by lunch and were cruising toward supper and having had only the pudding the nurses had provided, the twins were starving.

He should give Tory a little time to herself, but he knew she needed the twins to keep her grounded. So he let her unbuckle Sam from his car seat and carry him into the cottage.

"Our first order of business is to feed these two," he said, following her into the great room. He tossed his keys to the table behind the sofa.

"So you get their coats off while I heat up some baby food."

She nodded.

He raced to the kitchen and got food ready for the kids. One at a time, she removed a snowsuit then brought a baby to his or her highchair. When the food was ready, so were they.

Sam squealed with delight, showing off two new bottom teeth. Cindy laughed and patted her highchair tray.

"See? They're ready."

But Tory stood frozen by the chairs. She didn't even blink.

"Tory? A little help here?"

She peeked over at him. "Huh?"

"You feed Sam. I'll feed Cindy."

She took a step back, licked her lips.

"Okay." The empty expression on her face wasn't going away. She might be in the room, but she wasn't really present. And he didn't blame her. She'd been through a lot that day. "Why don't you go to your room? We'll be fine."

She nodded, pivoted and fled to her bedroom. He let her go, knowing that the love and cuddliness of two adorable babies could only go so far in terms of helping her broken heart.

But tomorrow morning, and the next morning and the next morning, they would be here for her. Ready to ease her back into her life.

And so would he.

He wouldn't let himself feel the relief of knowing they'd finally hit the point where he could help her for real. He wouldn't let himself think that his gain was another man's loss. He dealt only in reality. Fact. Figures. Because if he let himself think of Jason, lying in a hospital bed, breathing only with a machine, his emotions would overwhelm him. He wouldn't be able to help Tory.

So he didn't think of the vagaries of life, the unfairness of some things. He put his mind on helping Tory.

But a few hours later, he began to worry about her. She hadn't come out of her room for dinner. So he tapped on her bedroom door. If she didn't answer, he would assume she was sleeping, but if she did answer he wouldn't let her sit in her room and brood.

A very faint, "Yes," come from beyond her door.

So he opened it, stepped inside and found her packing. "What's up?"

"I'm going."

Half of him expected that. These next days would be the most difficult of her life and she might think she needed to be alone, but he knew she needed to be with him and their kids.

"Well, okay," he said, walking a little farther into the room. "I know you need some time and space, but there's no reason for you to leave."

"I need to be with Jason."

"I know that. You won't have to work for the next couple of days or weeks or whatever you need. But you're welcome here. We want to help you through this."

"Help *me* through this? Jason is the one who is dying."

He felt her slipping away. Not that he didn't want her to mourn Jason, not that he didn't want her to feel the sorrow she deserved, but he had the sudden, intense intuition that if he let her go, she'd never come back. "I know Jason is the one who is dying. But, Tory, just like always, you don't see that you're suffering too."

She took a careful step back. "I see. I always see. I'm just not the important one."

"I get it that Jason is the more important one now. I just don't want you to pull away so far that you forget you have us. We want you to stay with us."

"Stay with you?" Her face fell into sad lines. "How can I stay with the man I fell in love with while my fiancé was dying?"

CHAPTER FOURTEEN

CHANCE HONEST TO God thought his heart stopped. *She loved him?*

He wanted to pull her into his arms and kiss her until she was as breathless as he felt. But wasn't this the way of his life? He finally found the woman of his dreams, the one who made him happy to be alive, the one who made him believe that even though life was difficult, it could be fun. And when he learns she loves him he can't kiss her. He can't tell her he loves her. He can't say anything.

"I was supposed to stand by him. To be committed to him. And I fell in love with someone else."

He swallowed as diametrically opposed feelings pummeled him. His heart lightened to the point that it took his breath away, even as he felt the weight of knowing they were star-crossed.

Two people who'd met at the wrong time and were destined to fail.

But some optimistic part of him that still existed walked over to her. "You have never been anything but faithful. Don't do this to yourself." He set his hand on hers and stopped her from adding any more things to her suitcase. "Stay."

She pressed her lips together.

"Come eat dinner and then go to bed. We'll talk again in the morning."

He got her to eat some of the mashed potatoes and chicken Cook had sent down. Then, as if on autopilot, she walked to her room and closed the door. He checked on her around ten and found her fast asleep. He brushed her bangs from her face, kissed her forehead. He didn't know how they would get through the next days or weeks, but by God he would get them through.

The next morning she was awake, caring for the babies, when he staggered into the kitchen. She'd felt sorry enough for herself the day before and she wasn't going to do that again.

She also wouldn't put Chance through the

ringer. When he walked into the kitchen, she smiled and pointed at the coffeepot. "It's fresh."

"Thanks. Feeling better?"

"Yes." She lied. Not for herself but for Chance. She'd made a royal mess of this situation and she didn't know what to say or do. She'd made him feel guilty for her feelings for him and that wasn't right. She was the one who had fallen. It wasn't his fault. She would just keep her distance from here on out.

He turned from the counter with a cup of coffee and a slight smile. "Good."

She busied herself with the babies.

"Need any help?"

"No. We're fine."

He sucked in a breath and she prayed he wouldn't mention what she'd said the night before. Just as he'd decided after he'd kissed her the first time that it was better for them not to really talk, she knew that was what they had to do now.

"I have some work to do on the computer in my room. But if you need me, I'll come out."

Relief about buckled her knees. She said, "Great," as her cell phone rang.

She fished it out of her pocket and answered before it could ring again. “Hello.”

“It’s Nathan, sweetie.” He paused and drew in a shuddering breath. “Jason had a bad night last night. I think you need to come to the house.”

Her heart pounding, she closed the phone and bounced from her seat. “I need to go—”

“Go?”

She caught his gaze. “To Jason’s parents.”

“Okay, give me ten minutes to call Cook to babysit.”

She stopped him by laying her hand on his forearm. “I need to go alone.”

“But you need—”

“To go alone.”

Two hours later, he got the news that Jason had died. With the babies in the nursery sleeping, he threw a cup across the kitchen, smashing it against the wall.

“Chance—”

His mother’s voice drifted over the phone line, bringing him back to the present.

“The doctors I spoke with before I called you told me something very interesting.”

"Oh, yeah?" On the hospital board of directors, his mother had connections to everyone and everything related to the hospital. He certainly hoped she didn't think telling him that Jason's death was a blessing would cheer him up.

"They tell me that you and Tory took the twins to see him yesterday."

He rubbed his hand along the back of his neck. So, he wasn't going to get the blessing speech, but a scolding for taking the babies into the room of a dying man.

"The twins calmed her down." The defense slipped past his lips easily, naturally. He already had enough guilt about Jason to last him a lifetime. He didn't need something else.

"Oh, I know! One of the nurses monitored a lot of what happened in the room before the head nurse kicked you out." She took a breath. "The thing is, Jason didn't die this morning. They waited to call Tory so she'd have time to get some rest. He died a few minutes after your visit."

"What?" Grief swamped him. "They turned off his life support that soon?"

"That's just it. They didn't have to turn off his life support. He died on his own."

He might not be a brilliant man, but Chance knew that would be much easier on Tory. "He died right after we left?"

"Doctors know so little about head injuries and comas that they don't know what a person sees or hears, but one of them told me privately that your visit was a blessing. Sometimes people don't die because they worry about who'll care for their loved ones when they're gone. Your going into the room with Tory, bringing the babies, was almost like telling Jason that Tory had someone to take care of her."

He rubbed his hand along the back of his neck again, not sure what to say.

"You gave him the peace he needed to move on."

He hung up the phone feeling marginally better. Tory returned two hours later, so pale and bent that he wondered how she could support herself to walk. He hustled over to her, helped her to the sofa.

"Jason's parents called my mom."

She pressed her lips together as tears filled her eyes. "So you know."

"Yes."

He tried to pull her into his embrace, but she shrugged out of his hold. "How are the kids?"

"The kids are fine. Actually, they're with Mom."

Tory nodded as tears streamed down her face. Unable to bear seeing her like this, he caught her by the shoulders and forced her to face him. "I am so sorry."

Her tears turned to painful sobs. "He was so young. So smart. So everything."

Knowing she was remembering the boy she'd fallen in love with, Chance swallowed hard. "I'm sure he was."

"And funny. Nobody could make me laugh the way he could." She rose and paced away from the sofa. "And strong. I told you that I believe he'd somehow taken the brunt of that accident so that I'd be saved."

Chance swallowed again. Her pain was so intense it shimmered through the room. Hoping to comfort her, he said, "The doctors told my mom he passed away on his own."

She nodded.

He took a breath, "They also told her that Jason actually died a few minutes after our visit."

She pressed her lips together and nodded again in confirmation.

Relieved, he went on. “They said that sometimes people hang on because they worry about who’ll care for their loved ones. They think our visit with the twins was almost like telling Jason you had someone to take care of you.”

She sniffed a small laugh.

“So he could move on. He stayed until he knew you were going to be okay.”

“He would do that.”

Encouraged, Chance rose. “Yes. He would. Because he loved you and wanted you to be okay after he died.”

She said nothing.

“He just wants you to be okay.”

She turned suddenly. “*He* wants me to be okay? I think it’s you who wants me to be okay.”

He drew in a quick breath. “Of course, I do, but that doesn’t mean—”

She paced away from him. “I know you and everybody else think I should be grateful that his suffering is ended.” Her voice broke. “But I’m not. I’m so sad I honest to God feel that my heart is breaking.”

He took a step toward her. "Tory—"

She held up a hand to stop him. "Don't. Please. All this," she said, motioning around the great room. "Is very confusing right now. I should be grieving the man I adored. For ten years, he was the love of my life. And when he needed me the most I was here."

"You had to make a living."

"I was making a life." Her voice broke again. "Prematurely. Now, I need to grieve."

"And we'll give you all the space and time you need."

She shook her head furiously. "No! Don't you get it? I can't stay here. It only reminds me that while he was slipping away, I was too." She caught his gaze. "To you."

"Don't say that."

"It's true. We both know it's true."

"We did nothing—"

She gurgled in disgust. "We did *everything.* The important things. We broke my connection to him."

"No. We didn't. Both of us were very careful, very respectful of him."

She shook her head, then ran her hands down her face.

He took another step toward her. "And what we feel isn't foolish or tawdry." He considered his next words very carefully. She'd told him she loved him in the heat of anger when he couldn't answer her. Maybe it was time to fix that. "Because I love you too. Genuinely. With all my heart."

She closed her eyes then quickly opened them again and headed to her bedroom. Chance followed her, but she said nothing. Simply grabbed her nearly packed duffel bag and filled it.

Grief and a wild despair rattled through him. He'd told her he loved her and she had nothing to say? She was leaving?

His breathing froze as pain ricocheted through the chambers of his frantically beating heart. A million arguments raced through his head. Reasons she should stay. But if she wouldn't answer a declaration of love, what made him think anything he had to say was important to her?

He watched her walk through the great room, her shoulders slumped, her misery evident in every step. He told himself that she just needed time to sort all this out and once she'd had time she'd be back. Maybe not after the funeral. Maybe not in a few weeks. But after a month of working through everything that had happened, she'd be back.

But when the door closed behind her, he wasn't so sure.

For the second time in only a few months, Chance pulled his SUV through an intimidating black gate. This one at Saint John's Cemetery. A long string of cars with funeral flags on the hoods sat on the edge between the thin ribbon of road and the snow piled high beside it.

He didn't park at the end of the line. Instead, he stopped the SUV near a cluster of trees, got out and hoped his black topcoat allowed him to blend into the dark bark of the trees around him.

Mourners huddled under a small, tasteful tent that flapped in the winter wind. Chance spotted Tory immediately. With one of her father's arms wrapped around her and her mother holding her up on the other side, she sobbed pitifully.

His heart tumbled in his chest and he sucked in a breath. He had no idea what it felt like to love somebody so well, so completely that you'd bear the burden of five years of grief. No idea what it felt like to be that *loved.*

How can I stay with the man I fell in love with while my fiancé was in the hospital dying?

After her reaction to his declaration of love, he wondered if she even knew she'd said that.

That she loved him.

He listened to the minister, watched as the man closed his Bible then walked over to Jason's parents to give comfort before he stepped in front of Tory and handed her a rose. The minister spoke to her and hugged her, giving her special attention.

Chance swallowed hard. She'd spent the last five years a virtual prisoner. And he almost couldn't believe no one had paid her any notice until now. Not just because she was pretty but because something bright and good emanated from her.

And she loved him.

But she was racked with grief.

And because he'd been there, insinuating himself into her life for the past five months, telling her to move on, she might forever associate him with the final days of her fiancé.

The winter wonderland around him stilled and the thought of that shifted through him. That was the real reason she'd left him. He reminded her of the worst time in her life. A time she didn't want to remember, but forget.

That's why she wasn't with him. She wanted to forget him.

When the service was over, he quietly got into his car and drove home.

He stepped inside the cottage and Max and Kate both rose from the sofa, each holding a twin.

Max solemnly said, "Well?"

He shrugged out of his black topcoat. "She's devastated."

Kate sniffed back tears. "I can't even imagine."

"That's just it," he said, ambling over to the sofa. "I don't think any of us have a clue what she went through these past years."

"Is she coming back?"

He snorted. "Why? In the last months of her fiancé's life, we tried to draw her away from him. To make her laugh. To give her chances to grow, like encouraging her to go back to school. To make her forget her accident. If she doesn't hate me for that…and I'm pretty sure she does, we remind her of Jason. His last months." He plopped down on the sofa, and laid his head back so he was looking at the ceiling. "We remind her of the worst days of her life."

"Surely there were some good things—" Kate began.

But Max stopped her by laying his hand on her forearm. "Why don't you go up to the house and have Mom plan dinner for all of us tonight. We'll go home and get Clayton and Trisha. Then we can all have a nice, quiet dinner."

Kate glanced at Chance then back at Max. "Yes. That sounds like a good idea. Some family time."

When Kate was gone, Chance turned his head to the right and peered over at Max. "I'm not going to pour my heart out to you."

"I don't want you to pour your heart out. I just want you to listen. You might remind her of the worst days of her life, but there was something between you."

He snorted a laugh. "Right."

"You can't let that go."

"I also can't put her through any more than she's already been through."

"Chance, she's hurting now and she needs you. I let Kate go when she needed me the most and we lost eight years of our lives together. She went through a pregnancy alone, raised Trisha alone for eight years. You don't want to desert the woman you love when she needs you."

Chance shook his head. "When Kate needed you, she belonged to you. In some ways Tory still belongs to Jason. She might love me. She might need me. But I pushed her when she least needed to be pushed. I think that's why she ran away. So I won't do it again. I won't go after her. She has to come back to me."

Tory stayed in her room for the next two days. She didn't eat. She didn't sleep. On the third day, her mom came in with a breakfast tray and swished open the drapes covering the only window.

"Time to get up."

Tory groaned. "I've been up."

"I know. You've been up all night, sitting in the dark. It's time for that to be over."

"Not really. Not yet."

Samantha turned from the window. "I'm sorry, dear, but if you're taking classes in the spring, you have to enroll now."

She pulled the covers over her head. "I'm not ready."

"You have to be ready. Two weeks from now, when it's too late to enroll you'll be sorry."

She licked her lips. "I suppose."

"You might also want to call your boss."

Her gaze snapped up. "Chance?"

"Yes. You'll need money for classes. You have to work."

She swallowed. "Actually, I've saved enough to cover the first two semesters."

Her mom turned from the window. "So you're not going back to work?"

Her heart twisted. She could be with the twins right now. Happy.

She swallowed. She didn't want to be happy. It wasn't right to be happy. It wasn't right to go back to Chance's house and Chance's babies and Chance's arms, when Jason had just died.

Remembering how she'd been with him, how they'd kissed, how she'd longed to be able to love him, shame burned through her. She'd had five short months from the day she'd met Chance until her fiancé had died. She couldn't be patient for five short months?

"So, eat the eggs and toast I brought then get a shower and fix your hair and we'll take a ride over to the community college."

Tory looked at the tray of eggs and toast and her stomach flip-flopped. She thought of Valentine's Day. Chance making her breakfast in bed, pretending the kids had made it. Then Jason's parents arriving, telling her he'd had a stroke.

Her heart broke. "I don't think I need to eat."

"Please. Could you eat for me?"

She'd said the same thing to Sam the morning he was sick. Tears filled her eyes. She'd never see Jason again. She'd never see her babies again. She'd didn't want to see Chance again. Because somehow they'd all twisted together. And every time she thought of Chance, she thought of betraying Jason. And every time she thought of betraying Jason, she couldn't breathe. She couldn't think. All she could do was feel the horrible anvil of pain sitting on her chest.

"I'll eat this if you do me a favor."

"Anything."

"Call Gwen and tell her that I've quit. Tell her that Chance needs to hire another nanny."

"Oh, Tory. You should tell him in person."

"Really? I just lost Jason. I'm exhausted. I have to figure out the rest of my life. Can't I just once slide on something by having you call Gwen and settle this for me?"

Obviously surprised by her outburst, Tory's mom said, "Of course. I'm sorry."

Tory ran her hand along her forehead. "I'm sorry too."

And she was. Bitterly, bitterly sorry that she'd ruined so much.

Chance got the word that Tory had quit when Gwen came down with a file folder filled with the resumes. Once she'd heard Tory wasn't coming back, she'd called an agency and they'd emailed the information he'd need to choose a new nanny.

Chance looked at her. He knew in his heart she was doing what she considered to be the right thing. But he was tired and confused and angry that Tory couldn't even call him herself to quit. She'd had her mom call his mom.

Now he was looking at resumes? Just like that, Tory was out of his life?

"Leave the resumes," he said, rising from the sofa so his mom would too. "I'll look at them tonight."

"And get back to me with your choice in the morning?"

"Yes."

Pain sluiced through him. But if she noticed, Gwen didn't say anything. She grabbed her coat and left.

Standing in his living room, filled with a pain so intense it couldn't be described, he thought about what Max had said, about how he'd abandoned Kate when she'd needed him the most. Tired, confused, he scrubbed his hand across his mouth, then picked up the phone and dialed the first two digits of her cell phone—the number he'd saved when she called him from the hospital when Sam was sick—but he quickly hung up.

He did that four times that night, but in the end he just couldn't call her.

She'd told him she loved him in a tirade about her fear of hurting Jason, losing Jason. She'd pushed him away every chance she got. She'd fallen in love with him so reluctantly, that sometimes when he thought about it, it made his heart hurt.

And when he'd told her he loved her…she'd ignored him. Pretended she hadn't heard.

He couldn't go to her. If he went to her and she rejected him again, he'd be devastated. But he also knew he had to wait until she was ready.

She had to come to him.

CHAPTER FIFTEEN

THREE MONTHS LATER, sitting in Mrs. Mulcahy's accounting class, Tory looked in dismay at the simplistic spreadsheet she had created the week before. They were supposed to make a document that would assist them in creating a budget for a construction project, but though her formulas were correct, her headings left a lot to be desired.

She'd taken labor and materials into consideration, but when it came to materials her "guesstimates" were totally inaccurate. She'd forgotten little things like braces and brackets, tools and nails. Things Chance would have known about without a second thought.

Chance.

Her heart skipped a beat.

He loved her.

His actions had told her a million times over.

Tears filled her eyes and the numbers on the spreadsheet swam before her.

He'd trusted her with his kids. He'd paid attention to her, listened to her fears, respected her.

He'd taken her on the bike to help her get rid of her fears.

And he'd fallen in love with her and tempted her into being in love with him because he'd known, just as deep down inside she had known, that she was supposed to move on.

And she'd barely acknowledged any of the good things he'd done for her. She'd pushed him away. Every time they got too close, she'd pushed him away.

She swallowed as tears slipped down her cheeks.

She remembered shopping for the stroller, play yard and walkers. Remembered that he hadn't even known what a walker was.

She remembered their first kiss in the garden.

She remembered Christmas shopping for the babies.

She remembered breakfast in bed. The bear the twins had bought her for Valentine's Day.

And tears flowed even harder. The lengths he'd gone to to love her without hurting Jason amazed her. She hadn't actually noticed them at the time, but now everything was coming back to her in waves of memories—

Shooing her out of the house to visit Jason.

Taking her to see him after his stroke.

Bringing the kids too so she'd be grounded in reality.

She ran her hands down her face. Oh, God. What it must have done to him to have her simply ignore him when he told her he loved her.

In three long months, she hadn't let herself think about him and now she couldn't do anything but think about him.

She balled her spreadsheet into a wad and tossed it into a trash can, closed her book and rose from her desk.

"Miss Bingham!" Mrs. Mulcahy sputtered. "Where are you going?"

"Out."

"Are you ill?"

"Yes." That wasn't a lie. Now that her grieving had subsided and she was feeling better, she knew that how she'd handled the situation with Chance was wrong. After everything he'd felt for her and all the kindnesses he'd shown her, she'd just tossed him out of her life.

Like a selfish ninny.

She couldn't believe she'd been that thoughtless. That selfish. That self-absorbed. But she'd been grieving, so steeped in her loss and her pain she couldn't face him.

She had to make that up to him. At the very least, she had to apologize.

Chance stood by a screen displaying his PowerPoint presentation for the board of directors for Montgomery Development, with Max sitting at the head of the table in his capacity as chairman.

"In a project billed as community development, we don't expect to make a profit, but the goodwill we'll earn with the contractors we employ will be worth its weight in gold."

His cell phone buzzed in his jacket pocket, but he ignored it and went on discussing the pros and cons of bidding on a huge local renovation that wouldn't make them a dime. Still it was exactly the kind of project they had been looking for to use as a payback for the community.

His cell phone buzzed again and this time he reached into his pocket and turned it off.

Max said, "Have you worked out the projection for—"

The phone on the conference room table rang. The receptionist's voice came over the speaker. "I'm sorry, Mr. Montgomery. But your mother is on line one. She said it's urgent."

Max reached for the phone, but Chance beat him to it. "She's a quarter of a mile away from the kids. Something might have happened to one of them."

He yanked the phone out of the cradle. "Mom?"

"Chance, darling, you have to come home."

His heart stopped. "Why? What happened? Are the kids okay?"

"The kids are okay, but I need you—"

"Mom, I'm in the middle of a meeting."

"Chance, have you ever known me to swear?"

"No."

"Then the words 'get your ass home' should be sufficient for you to realize I'm serious."

With that she hung up. Max said, "What's going on?"

"She told me to get my ass home."

Max winced. "Then you'd better get home."

He tried not to break any speed laws as he raced

along the downtown streets and up the hill to the wealthy part of town. But he knew, he just *knew*, something was wrong with one of the twins, and she didn't want to tell him over the phone.

Even before he got to the front door, it opened. His mother said, "Go into the study."

"Where are the kids?"

"They're at your house with Bridget," she said, referring to the new nanny.

He frowned. "Then why did you call me?"

She turned him and physically shoved him. "Go!"

He stumbled a bit after her shove, then made his way back to the hall expecting to find a gift. His mother had bought him new furniture, new suits, a new car, all in the name of getting him settled in town, but he knew she was aiming to get him over the hurdle of losing Tory. It hadn't worked. Time had healed a couple of the wounds. But there were days he still missed her. Which was why he wouldn't be surprised to find a real estate agent sitting on the leather sofa with a folder full of listings to show him.

With a sigh, he opened the door.

And saw Tory.

He faltered. Part of him wanted to run to her. The other part knew she could be here just to apologize for running out on him and the kids. She was kind like that. Responsible. And wouldn't he be a fool to race into her arms only to have her rebuff him again, and have to start the healing process all over?

She turned at the sound of the door and her face gave away nothing. A thin straight line, her lips were neither smiling nor frowning. Soft with sadness, her big brown eyes caught his gaze.

"Hi."

He took a step inside the door. "Hi."

"You look good."

He smiled. "Handmade suits from Italy will make any guy look good."

She sniffed a laugh. "Right. You know you're attractive."

He did, but he also knew that good looks could get a guy in as much trouble as they could get him favors. And his good looks hadn't been enough to keep her. They'd been enough to tempt her, but not to keep her.

He took another cautious step into the room. He trusted himself not to fall at her feet, but just barely. He needed to come out of at least one exchange with her with his dignity.

"You're not bad yourself. So you can't be pointing fingers."

She laughed, and his heart skipped a beat. He'd heard her laugh a hundred times, but never when it came to the two of them, to their attraction, to anything that might remotely link them.

He took another step. "You seem okay."

"I am okay. Really okay." Her eyes misted. "I've had a very, very difficult six years."

He took another step into the room. "Those were more than difficult years. They were tragic. Some days I wondered how you survived."

"Some days I did too."

Her soft voice brought tears to his eyes. He'd always felt a tad sorry for himself, for his parentage, his dad's lies, but standing only a few feet away from a person who'd really suffered, he knew he'd lived a blessed life.

"But you're okay now."

She smiled. "Yeah." She sucked in a breath. "I'm taking classes at the community college."

"It's what you'd said you wanted." She was moving on. Just as he knew she should. And though he should be glad, a part of him felt torn in two. He wished she'd say what she'd come here to say, so he could leave, brood again over her loss, and then maybe *he* could get on with *his* life.

He wouldn't get his hopes up again.

Tory watched him walking into the room slowly, hesitantly and knew he hadn't gotten over the hurt she'd inflicted when she left him.

So she said the words she'd come here to say. "I'm so sorry."

He smiled. Relief filled her. Still, she hadn't left her classes to clear her own conscience. She'd wanted to see him to make *him* feel better. "I mean it, Chance. You were nothing but good to me. You were the only person who really saw what I was going through." She hesitated and caught his gaze. "I appreciate that."

He looked away. "I think it might have been one of those misery loves company things."

"Or maybe misery recognizes misery."

He shrugged.

"Nobody even took the time to notice that I was on the edge. My parents wanted me to get a job. Jason's parents wanted me at the personal care facility, as if my presence proved he was still alive."

"I can understand both."

"Yet, you were the one who didn't push me."

He laughed. "I gave you two babies to care for. And instead of hanging around to help, I went to Montgomery Development every day, even before Max nudged me into taking the job."

"I didn't care." She waited until he glanced at her again before she said, "I loved the babies. I loved caring for them. They sort of made me feel alive again."

He smiled and nodded.

She sucked in a breath. "You made me feel alive again too."

"Alive enough to feel guilty."

"It was a difficult situation."

"Which is why I accept your apology and totally understand everything."

She got the message. He wanted her to leave. Her mission accomplished, she would go. But first she memorized the pretty blue of his eyes, the slope of his cheeks, his defined chin. She never wanted to forget him.

Her heart stumbled in her chest. She *didn't* want

to forget him. She didn't want to *leave* him. She didn't want to lose him.

But from the serious set of his face, she knew she already had.

Still—

Her gaze locked with his, she twisted her hands, wondering what he'd say if she said, "I love you."

His eyes flickered.

"I always have." With her heart pounding in her chest, she couldn't stop herself from going on. "I tried so hard to fight it. I tried so hard to tell myself that I was lonely and sad and that's why you were so tempting. But I was only kidding myself. I genuinely love you. And you need to know that."

He swallowed and took a step back.

Remorse rumbled through her, but she stopped it. All those months that he'd been so good to her, loving her with no reward, no recompense, earned him the right to know the truth even if he no longer loved her.

Finally, he said, "You love me?"

She straightened. "Yes." She smiled ruefully. "I spent the past three months trying to return to real life and this morning you popped into my head and I knew no matter what I said or what I did or how we'd come together, I loved you."

Standing by his mother's desk, he looked down and traced a finger on the edge.

The silent room did nothing to ease Tory's nerves and she wondered why she was standing there. What was she waiting for? For him to tell her that he loved her? She'd ruined that. He'd told her he loved her and she ignored him. He wouldn't be so foolish as to still love her after that. It was time to go.

She headed for the door. "I'll leave now. I just wanted you to know that I was sorry." She paused, faced him again. "And to know that I loved you."

With a quick pivot, she resumed her walk to the door.

"Stop."

She hesitated then turned.

He sighed and glanced around the semidark room, made darker by the brown leather furniture and heavy cherrywood desk and chair. "Our timing sucks."

Her heart about beating out of her chest, she

forced herself to stay quiet, fearful that she'd push him into saying something he didn't want to say.

He walked toward her and impatience overtook her. She took the few steps to meet him in the middle. When they were close enough, he took her hands. "I love you. I've loved you since you introduced me to walkers, got the kids to sleep all night and looked at me as if I was the best-looking guy you'd ever seen."

She laughed, but her throat also closed. Their romance had never been about hearts and flowers. It had been about babies and breakfast, getting up at night for each other, and an earthy attraction that caused them both to fumble.

"I like the fact that you made me feel normal."

"You're not normal." He tugged on her hands to bring her close. "You're beautiful."

She laughed.

"Oh, you laugh. You tormented me for months and now you won't let me be romantic?"

Her heart burst with love. "Go ahead. Be romantic."

"Okay." His voice dropped to a mere whisper. "You're beautiful and strong. Breathtakingly sexy and alluring." He moved his hands from her wrists up her arms and then down her back. "And I can't wait to get you into bed."

She laughed. "That's not romantic."

"The hell it isn't."

He kissed her then and finally, finally, she didn't have to fear. No guilt assaulted her. All she felt was pleasure…and joy…and happiness so strong she thought she'd burst from it.

When they finally pulled back, she plucked at his tie. "So, do you think I can have my old room back?"

"You want to be my nanny?"

"I want to be the babies' mom."

"Well, that means you have to sleep with the babies' dad and you're definitely not going to be his employee." He tightened his hold on her waist. "I have a better idea."

She peeked up at him. "You do?"

"Yeah, I think we should date."

She laughed. "Date?"

"You know, you and me, movie, popcorn. A dinner out here and there. Romantic weekends at bed and breakfasts." He nuzzled into her neck. "Maybe a trip to the Virgin Islands every winter."

The touch of his lips sent a shiver through her.

"Just exactly how long do you think we're going to date?"

"Forever."

She nudged his shoulders and forced him to look at her. "Oh, no, you don't. You're making an honest woman of me."

"Well, I was thinking we could even date after we got married. We were sort of cheated, you and I. So why not enjoy it?"

Why not indeed?

"So what's first?"

He slid his arm around her waist. "I was thinking iced tea on the patio behind the cottage. Maybe a movie tonight." He opened the door and led her up the hall toward the foyer, where Gwen stood wringing her hands. "Some popcorn. A little time with the kids. And then I'll drive you home and kiss you senseless in the car outside your parents' house."

She laughed.

Gwen said, "So?"

"So, we're happy."

Tory smiled. "We're happy."

Gwen sighed with relief. "Oh, thank God. I've got an entire staff gathered in the kitchen worrying. If you'd come out crying," she said, pointing at Tory. "Or you'd come out angry," she added, pointing at Chance. "I never would have had this house ready for Sunday's barbeque."

She headed for the kitchen, clapping her hands. "All right everybody. Work stoppage is over. I'll have Tory print a newsletter and you can read all about it."

Chance laughed. "Are you ready for this? I mean, my life isn't easy and Gwen's kind of a nut—"

She smiled up at him. "I've never been more ready."

EPILOGUE

A YEAR AND A HALF later, Chance stood in front of the altar, at the end of a long aisle, Max at his side. Dressed in a rose-colored dress, Trisha had already walked down the satin-and-rose-petal walkway, and stood in front of the first pew. Holding a bouquet as she tried to corral Cindy and Sam, Kate was next.

She wore the same color and style dress as Trisha and so did the little peanut—two-and-a-half-year-old Cindy. The cap sleeve slid off her tiny shoulder and her little legs peeked out from beneath a knee-length skirt that was nothing but ruffles. She happily waved to the people in the pews who tittered behind their hands, their eyes shining as they watched the tuxedo-clad little boy and attention-loving little girl make their way down the aisle.

Then the music stopped, paused dramatically,

before the organist broke into "Here Comes the Bride."

And his heart stopped, paused dramatically, when Tory and her dad appeared at the door.

In a rustle of white skirts, she and her dad, a proud papa grinning like a Cheshire cat, started down the aisle.

But Chance's eyes were glued on Tory. In the past year, she'd finished community college, and they'd begun to date. Even now he smiled at the memory. Neither one of them had dated in so long they almost didn't know how, but loving each other had come easily.

So easily.

And now she was here. *His.*

His chest tightened with joy.

Her big brown eyes sparkled back at him as she approached. His gazed drifted down to the pretty white gown, strapless and shimmering, it molded to her sleek body, riding the curve of her waist, hugging her shapely hips and sliding down her thighs until it hit her knees. Then it belled out several rows of ruffles that looked like—

She got closer.

His eyes narrowed.

Feathers?

The skirt of her dress was feathers? He laughed out loud. Not that the feathers looked funny. They didn't. Soft and shimmery, they enhanced the beauty of the dress. But they were fun.

Like she was.

She might be sweet. She might even be a wonderful, serious mother. But she had a silly side. A fabulous, hysterical silly side that, he believed, had actually gotten them both beyond Jason's death.

She finally reached him and he took her hand from her father's.

Then they turned and faced the altar and said their vows.

To love and cherish.

Respect each other.

Until death do they part.

The ceremony ended. Pictures, thanks to the dictations of his mother and Tory's, took an hour. Finally, finally, they herded into limos and headed for the reception. When they reached the country club, he helped Tory and her feathery gown out of the limo.

She smiled up at him, leaned against him and kissed him.

"I love you."

"I love you too."

The photographer pointed to a gazebo and started giving instructions about even more pictures.

Kate, Trisha, Tory and even Cindy hurried to follow his directions.

But Chance held back. He wasn't needed anyway. The photographer first wanted to get tons of pictures of Tory and the bridesmaids.

Content, he leaned against the black limo, listened to the happy birds, watched his bride and his daughter pose for pictures....

But an abrupt, unexpected "something" filled the air. Almost as if someone was talking to him.

He glanced around. The peace and privacy of the exclusive country club surrounded him.

He started to relax but the feeling returned. This time stronger.

He glanced at happy Tory, and suddenly knew what was nagging him.

He looked up at the blue, blue sky. "I don't know where you are." He grimaced. "It feels like you're right here. Beside me. But I don't care. You can shadow me forever." He sucked in a breath. "I owe you. Not for dying, but for saving her. She believes you saved her that day on the bike, and I believe her." He swallowed hard. "So thanks."

The unexpected feeling intensified. He whipped around, glanced at Tory again, posing with his baby girl and little bruiser son.

He looked up at the sky again. "I adore her. If you're waiting for me to say I'll take good care of her, I'm saying it. I will take very, very good care of her."

A breeze swirled around him. As quickly as it came up, it disappeared.

And the feeling of Jason was gone.

Someone tapped him on the shoulder. He turned and found Tory. "Hey. Pictures, remember?"

Unable to resist, he pulled her to him and kissed her, long and deep as if he might not ever get the chance to kiss her again.

"What was that for?"

"A promise."

"Another one? Didn't we make enough of those at the altar?"

"Yeah. But this is a special one." He brushed her bangs across her forehead. "I'm going to take very, very good care of you."

She smiled. "I know." Her smile grew. "I've always known."

"Me too."

He shoved away from the limo. Tory held out her hand to him and he took it—intending to keep every promise he'd made.

* * * * *

BANISHED TO THE HAREM
Carol Marinelli

NOT JUST THE GREEK'S WIFE
Lucy Monroe

A DELICIOUS DECEPTION
Elizabeth Power

PAINTED THE OTHER WOMAN
Julia James

TAMING THE BROODING CATTLEMAN
Marion Lennox

THE RANCHER'S UNEXPECTED FAMILY
Myrna Mackenzie

NANNY FOR THE MILLIONAIRE'S TWINS
Susan Meier

TRUTH-OR-DATE.COM
Nina Harrington

A GAME OF VOWS
Maisey Yates

A DEVIL IN DISGUISE
Caitlin Crews

REVELATIONS OF THE NIGHT BEFORE
Lynn Raye Harris

0113 Rom LP

A NIGHT OF NO RETURN
Sarah Morgan

A TEMPESTUOUS TEMPTATION
Cathy Williams

BACK IN THE HEADLINES
Sharon Kendrick

A TASTE OF THE UNTAMED
Susan Stephens

THE COUNT'S CHRISTMAS BABY
Rebecca Winters

HIS LARKVILLE CINDERELLA
Melissa McClone

THE NANNY WHO SAVED CHRISTMAS
Michelle Douglas

SNOWED IN AT THE RANCH
Cara Colter

EXQUISITE REVENGE
Abby Green

BENEATH THE VEIL OF PARADISE
Kate Hewitt

SURRENDERING ALL BUT HER HEART
Melanie Milburne